PARANORMAL COZY MYSTERY

# Heists & Poltergeists

## TRIXIE SILVERTALE

Sittin' On A Goldmine
Productions L.L.C.

Sittin' On A Goldmine Productions, L.L.C.

info@sittinonagoldmine.co

www.sittinonagoldmine.co

Publisher's note: This is a work of fiction. Names, characters, places and incidents are products of the author's imagination or are used fictitiously and are not to be construed as real. Any resemblance to actual events, locales, organizations, or persons, living or dead, is entirely coincidental.

ISBN: 978-1-952739-78-1

Cover Design © Sittin' On A Goldmine Productions, L.L.C.

Trixie Silvertale
Heists and Poltergeists: Paranormal Cozy Mystery : a novel / by Trixie Silvertale — 1st ed.
[1. Paranormal Cozy Mystery — Fiction. 2. Cozy Mystery — Fiction. 3. Amateur Sleuths — Fiction. 4. Female Sleuth — Fiction. 5. Wit and Humor — Fiction.] 1. Title.

Have you ever had the feeling something is about to be very wrong? I'm not talking about a passing thought that slips through your brain and disappears. I'm referring to that undeniable shiver deep in your gut.

Well, I'm having one right now. I'm standing in line at the bank, staring at the wig on the lady in front of me—and boom.

Tummy shivers and hairs stand on end on the back of my neck.

It's nothing against the wig. I have a drawer full of them back in the apartment I share with the ghost of my deceased grandmother.

As I'm about to dismiss the thought as a potentially misguided psychic hit triggered by the woman's elaborate garb, the antique mood ring on my left hand encircles my finger in an icy chill. Glancing at the swirly black mist inside the smoky cabochon, an image struggles to appear. But then . . .

BANG!

"This is a robbery!"

Everything seems to slow down, and I feel as though my ears are stuffed with cotton. I don't remember crouching, but I suppose that was an instinctual reaction to the gunshot.

Turning toward the sound, I'm surprised to see the White Rabbit standing on top of Tilly's desk, waving a handgun. Before I can marvel at the cartoon-like mask and fuzzy white ears, the Queen of Hearts, in all her Wonderland glory, hops over the counter and begins tearing cash out of drawers as a terrified bank teller attempts to keep her hands in the air, and simultaneously open said drawers.

Guarding the exit is none other than a shotgun-toting Mad Hatter, with a wild wig and a crooked top hat covering his real hair.

Could this day *get* any weirder?

Just when I'm about to be disappointed that the guest of honor is missing . . . Alice, of Wonderland fame, sporting her signature blonde locks, and the Cheshire Cat come in through a hallway that must originate at a rear entrance from the alley behind the bank.

I may be in the middle of a dangerous armed robbery, but the film-school dropout inside me experiences a moment of intense satisfaction that the Wonderland tea party is complete.

Of course, the entire time I'm swirling around in my mind movies, the White Rabbit has been informing the handful of patrons and employees what to do to avoid being shot.

Oops. That was probably kinda useful information, but I'm getting ahead of myself.

Let's start at the beginning . . .

CHAPTER 1

WHOEVER INVENTED THE BIRTHDAY MANTRA "my day, my way" has never met Grams. I mean, who would've thought the ghost of my dearly departed grandmother could wreak so much havoc in my life?

Not me.

You live—then you live with a bossy ghost—and you learn.

I've learned a lot of wonderful things since a malodorous bus dropped me farther north than I'd ever traveled in my life. My grandmother's dying wish, to find her missing granddaughter and leave her a mountain of cash and an amazing bookshop brimming with ancient magic-filled tomes, has afforded me a lifestyle I never could've imagined.

Back when I was slinging coffee and living

without hot water in my sketchy studio apartment in Sedona, not even the most skilled pseudo-shamans in the Southwest could've manifested the idea of a place like Pin Cherry Harbor.

Not to get sidetracked, but I'm sure there were some legit shamans in Vortex-ville. I just never happened to serve coffee to any of them.

Back to the dilemma *du jour*. It will be my twenty-fourth birthday in three short days. Ever since a terrible accident took my mother shortly after my eleventh birthday, the day of my arrival into this world stopped being something to celebrate. As I bounced my way through a series of unimpressive foster homes, I learned to scale my hopes way back. There were no cakes, there were no presents, and there certainly were no parties.

So, when I arrived in almost-Canada and had the bejeezus scared out of me by the ghost of Myrtle Isadora, and the bonus discovery of a living father, it never occurred to me to mention my birth-date to either of them. Which, for the record, is March 21st, the first day of spring.

Please don't explain to me how the position of the sun dictates the vernal equinox, and how the date shifts based on astronomical variables. If we're going to be friends, and I hope we are, you need to get on board with this thing I have about my birthday. March 21$^{st}$. First day of spring. My birthday. End of story.

Due to my error of omission, my first birthday here passed without a trace, and the second birthday extravaganza had to be abandoned due to my grandmother's spirit suffering temporary cursed imprisonment in a pendant—as the result of a decades-long feud with a local gypsy. But that's a different story.

Welcome to this year! Grams' spirit is once again free to roam the bookshop at will, she's able to summon the strength to hold a pen for great lengths of time, and she spends each and every day making to-do lists for the people in her inner circle of surprise party planners.

Spoiler alert: I'm a psychic. Trying to surprise a psychic is a plan doomed to fail.

However, because of my deep and abiding affection for Ghost-ma, I've pretended for several months to be unaware of their surreptitious activities.

Now the massive celebration is looming, and I'm not sure I'm prepared to step into the megawatt spotlight she's certainly rented.

I need to calm my nerves and indulge in some comfort food, and there's no better place to do that than the diner owned by my grandmother's first husband, Odell Johnson.

"I'm heading off to the diner, Grams."

No response. At least I can breathe a sigh of relief that she wasn't close enough to be thought-dropping.

"Last chance to be disappointed in my outfit—"

"Ree-ow." Soft but condescending.

"Hey, Pyewacket. Are you filling in for Grams?" I bend to scratch his broad tan head between his black-tufted ears.

"Reow." Can confirm. His short, thick tail flicks left and right.

"Well, you're doing her proud, son."

He silently leads the way to the back room and swats his empty bowl at me with one large, needle-clawed paw.

"I wouldn't dream of leaving without feeding you." Grabbing a box of his favorite sugary children's cereal from the cupboard, I heap his bowl and step back. I learned quickly that this half-wild caracal does not tolerate affection at mealtime.

As I place a hand on the alley door—

"Mizithra! Were you going to leave without saying goodbye?" The shimmering spirit places a bejeweled hand on one hip and straightens her burgundy silk-and-tulle Marchesa gown with the other.

"No need for formal names, Grams. I called out a farewell, and got nothing but radio silence. I figured you were hard at work on your memoirs."

"Oh, that makes sense, dear. I was busy with—"
Her ghostly eyes widen and her perfectly drawn brows lift.

"With what?" Purposely holding a blank space in my head—a recently perfected skill—I wait.

"I'm not sure I like this new 'skill,' sweetie." Ghost-ma purses her lips and shakes her head.

"Of course you don't. You normally spend half your time snooping around in my private thoughts. I may not know how to keep you out, but I can make sure the shelves are bare when you're poking around. Maybe you'll be able to finish your memoirs with all this extra time."

"Well, I never!" She clutches at one of her many strands of pearls.

Opening the door, I step into the slushy alley and toss a familiar refrain over my shoulder. "I think we both know that's not true, Myrtle Isadora Johnson Linder Duncan Willamet Rogers!"

As the door bangs, I hear one last ethereal request. "Say hello to Odell for me."

That would be the "Johnson" in the long list of former husbands' surnames.

THE MARCH WEATHER is still draped in icicles and stirred by frosty breezes swirling across the great lake nestled in our harbor. Despite the short walk from my bookshop to Myrtle's Diner, the gust of warm air that greets me as I step inside the hallowed eatery is eagerly welcomed.

Slipping off my mittens, I wave to my grandfather and inhale the scent of potato products and java. He gives me the standard spatula salute through the red-Formica-trimmed orders-up window.

That's my cue to slide into a booth and accept the steaming mug of go-go juice that is almost instantly delivered by the world's most amazing waitress, Tally.

"How's your week shaping up, Mitzy?"

This would be her thinly veiled attempt to see if I have any knowledge of the pending surprise party. I've fielded a number of these questions in the last couple of weeks. "No big plans. Just going to stay indoors and keep warm. I hear there's a storm on the way."

She smiles, satisfied that I'm still in the dark about the big doings. "Well, good for you." Her flame-red bun bobs up and down as she hustles from booth to table, refilling coffee cups and chewing the fat.

Having a favorite restaurant and enjoying a cup of coffee I didn't have to make myself—with yesterday's grounds—are luxuries I still appreciate every day. A long sip of the diner's delicious black gold warms me from the inside out.

The only thing that could improve on this perfect moment—

A whoosh of cold air delivers a shiver and a tingle, as Sheriff Too-Hot-To-Handle strides through the diner's door and into my scene.

My inner film director is over the moon with this perfect timing. Since the two of us are well acquainted, I can't actually call this our "meet cute," but dagnabbit if that man isn't adorable.

His cheeks flush with color when he catches me sizing him up like a chocolate croissant, and he stomps the snow off his work boots before joining me in the booth.

"Morning, Mitzy. I'm surprised to find you here."

My jaw sags and my eyes widen, but then I catch sight of his teasing grin. "Ha ha, Sheriff. If you're trying to make me feel bad about eating at my grandfather's restaurant four or five days out of seven, it's not going to work. My whole thing is 'family first.'"

Erick chuckles as he removes his shearling-lined uniform jacket and tucks it onto the seat. "I think you meant to say, french fries first."

"Rude."

He smooths down his long, slicked-back blond bangs, walks his fingers across the table, and turns his palm upward. It's a move he stole from my repertoire, but I hold no grudge. I slide my hand into his and we both smile stupidly as he squeezes my fingers.

In a weak attempt to deflect the fry comment, I mention, "For your information, it's well before noon and—"

Odell approaches the table and slides my usual scrambled eggs with chorizo and a bottle of Tabasco sauce in front of me. "Your pancakes will be out in a minute, Sheriff."

Erick nods.

Regulars like Erick Harper and I have no need to order. The owner has a very special knack for knowing exactly what his patrons need. Odell raps his knuckles twice on the silver-flecked white Formica table and returns to the grill.

"Did you hear about the storm?" I wink at Erick and squeeze his hand. There's nothing locals enjoy more than discussing the weather—or so I've learned.

He rubs his thumb along my fingers and smiles. "There's no storm coming. What makes you say that?"

"Wishful thinking, I suppose."

"Last I checked, you weren't a fan of cold

weather. What on earth would make you wish for a storm that would prolong your suffering?"

"First of all, winter is growing on me. I may not be a fan of freezing, but I've learned to enjoy several snow-based activities."

Before I can get to my second point, he jumps in. "Is one of those activities discovering corpses?"

What can I say? The man has a point. "You're not wrong. However, I was referring to things like cross-country skiing, snowmobiling, cutting my own Christmas tree . . . You get the idea."

He shrugs. "If memory serves, you discovered a dead body during each of those endeavors." Laughter shakes his shoulders and I'm forced to hang my head in mute agreement.

"Listen, I don't go looking for trouble. Somehow, it seems to find me."

Erick leans back, yawns, and stretches his muscular arms as he nods in agreement. "You don't have to convince me, Moon. There's something about you, and one day I'm going to figure out what it is."

The friendly banter ends. The crux of our current dilemma rears its ugly head before his pancakes have a chance to arrive. Secrets.

I endured more than my share of teasing during childhood. My strange, bone-white hair and almost colorless grey eyes led to an enormous amount of taunting. Of course, my orphan backstory offered plenty of ammunition as well. Once I escaped the foster system and struggled to make it on my own, I had one mission: fit in. If people wanted to party, I partied the hardest. If the dare was to climb on the statue of a horse and take a selfie, I was first in line. The role of ringleader was always preferable to outsider.

Now I have this crazy set of psychic gifts that truly do make me a form of freakish—not to mention my budding skills as an alchemist—and I'm terrified to let the truth out. Erick is no dummy. He knows there's more to my hunches than I'm letting on, and it's causing some serious friction in our relationship.

Suddenly I'm aware of long, sexy fingers wiggling in front of my face and a soft voice whispering, "Mitzy. Oh, Mitzy Moon. Are you in there?"

Oh brother. In addition to my psychic situation, I have a terrible habit of retreating to a world housed solely within my mind. I found a great deal of comfort there as a child, but the habit is a bit off-putting to most adults. "I was sort of running through my to-do list for the day." Lame. He's never going to buy that.

He sits back, grabs a forkful of his syrupy blueberry pancakes, which must've arrived while I was catatonic, and shoves it in his mouth.

I can't believe he didn't have a snappy comeback. Fine. Two can play this game. I shove golden-brown home fries in my mouth and stare back at him with a serious "game on" vibe.

Erick takes a swig of his coffee and smiles. "I'd love to get a peek at that to-do list. Let me see how close I can get. Item 1: eat breakfast at my grandfather's restaurant. Item 2: walk back to my bookshop. Item 3: . . ." He gazes up at the ceiling and comically taps his chin, as though he's deep in thought. "Boy, I'm having trouble coming up with number three."

I'd love to tell him I plan to spend the rest of the day avoiding my grandmother and her thinly veiled party plans, but I know he's a member of the surprise team and I don't want to spoil their fun. "Actually, Sheriff, my little stepbrother, Stellen, and I have some 'get in a car and drive' plans."

He wipes the drip of syrup off his lickable lips and smiles. "Oh, I forgot he was home on spring break. How's he doing?"

"In school? He's crushing it. But emotionally he's struggling. He wants to go to the cemetery and visit his parents' graves, so that part is a bit of a downer."

Erick nods. "Yeah, the kid's had it pretty tough. I'm sure glad your dad and Amaryllis adopted him. He deserves some good things in his life, you know?"

"Copy that. Plus, I can visit Isadora's headstone and leave some flowers or something."

We share a confused look.

I shrug. "Is that weird?" Leaning forward, I whisper, "I never think of visiting her grave because I see her every day. But normal people put flowers on graves, right?"

His dreamy, blue eyes spark with a dare. "Yes, *normal* people do."

CHAPTER 2

IN SITUATIONS WHERE my back is against the wall
and I'm out of options, I tend to rely on dark humor
or my barely passable acting skills. Here goes
nothing . . . and, ACTION! "Shoot! I'm gonna have
to take this food to go. I'm supposed to meet
Stellen." Before Erick can react, I slide out of the
booth and grab a to-go box from behind the counter.

Returning to the table, I pack up my half-eaten
breakfast, as he shoves pancakes into his mouth
with unnecessary force.

"See you later. I'll try not to stumble across any
corpses." The false cheeriness of my tone is sur-
passed only by the imitation brightness of my smile.
As I lean down to place a quick kiss on his rugged
jaw, I catch his mumbled come back.

"Sounds like a tall order if you're headed to the cemetery."

I turn up the wattage on my smile, wave to my grandfather, and rush out of the diner without a backward glance.

Yes, I feel bad about bailing on that conversation for the umpteenth time, but I've seen all the movies, I've watched all the television shows. When the girlfriend reveals her strange powers, it never ends well.

Maybe I'm a chicken. But also, maybe I'm a genius. If I can avoid the topic and act normal, there's a chance this whole suspicion thing will blow over. I don't have to get *hunches*. I don't have to solve crimes. I came to Pin Cherry on a whim and stayed because of relationships, not sleuthing.

When I told Erick that family was the most important thing to me, I wasn't making that up. So, starting today, I'm going to turn over a new leaf. I'm going to mind my own business, and keep my extrasensory perceptions to myself. Like he always says, the sheriff's department was solving crimes before I came to town. Seems like there's no reason they can't keep solving them without my help.

The tension in my shoulders vanishes, and, despite the icy wind, a sensation of warmth spreads through my body. I have a brilliant plan, and I get to spend the day with my brother. He could use the support, and I can absolutely use the distraction.

Instead of heading into the bookshop, I turn left on First Avenue, walk straight past the Bell, Book & Candle Bookshop, and continue to the alley that separates my store from my father's restorative justice offices and penthouse living quarters.

I have a key, because that's how my family rolls, so I let myself in and take the elevator to the top floor.

PING.

Two sets of eyes turn toward the sliding doors, but Amaryllis is the first to grin broadly and rush toward me. "Mitzy!"

Next thing I know, she's hugging me tightly, patting me on the back, and offering me a cup of coffee—which I politely decline—all at the same time. If this woman is anywhere near as good a lawyer as she is a hostess—opposition beware.

Stellen takes the calmer approach to my arrival and offers me a cool-guy fist bump, one-armed hug combo. "Hey, Mitzy."

"Hey, yourself. Are you ready to head out?"

He glances at Amaryllis, looks down at the ground, and shoves his hands deep inside the pockets of his jeans.

I hardly need my special abilities to sense

there's a problem. "What's up? Did you change your mind?"

Amaryllis squeezes her hands together, tilts her head to the side, and exhales loudly. "He's having second thoughts. He forgot it was your birthday week, and now he thinks it's in poor taste to drag you out to a cemetery."

My face scrunches up in confusion as I shake my head. "Birthday *week*? Are you nuts? This isn't about me. You're hardly ever in town, and Dad already told me you're planning on doing some kind of summer-school program . . . This is important to you. I'm your sister. Granted, I'm pretty new at the job, but I think this is one of the things I'm supposed to do. It's, like, Big Sister 101, right?"

His hair has grown inches since I last saw him and long black curls hang across most of his face. He tucks them behind one ear and his bright-green eyes gaze up at me with hope. "You sure? I could go by myself."

"Look, bro, I haven't celebrated a birthday DAY, let alone a week, since I was eleven, so I kind of forget it's even a thing. Hanging out with you is what's important to me. I know how much moms matter. Your mother's death may have been expected, because of her illness, but that doesn't mean it's been any easier to deal with. This coping business is something we share, all right?"

He nods. "Let me get my stuff."

Stellen disappears down the hallway toward his room, and I catch Amaryllis wiping a tear from the corner of her eye. "It's really sweet of you, honey. I know it can't be easy for you."

"Hey, when his father was killed and you and dad stepped up, I knew I had to do the same. He's such a great kid. It makes it easy."

Now there's a tear leaking from the corner of my eye, and Amaryllis wraps me in another one of her signature bear hugs. For a petite woman, she has the strength of a championship wrestler.

Stellen emerges from his room with a piece of paper in one hand, and a small stuffed squirrel holding an acorn.

"Did you—"

He lifts the squirrel and turns it back and forth. "He died of natural causes on the campus. You know my dad was always disappointed I didn't take up the family taxidermy business. I figured he'd appreciate the gesture."

"You really are the best kid, buddy. What's the slip of paper?"

His eyes glisten with unshed tears. "My report card."

And, in that moment, I feel as though we share one soul. Back in elementary school, when I still cared about grades, I would've given anything for my mother to see my report card and tell me how smart I was. Something unspoken passes between us, and he rubs his eyes furiously.

He places the items on the counter, slips into his jacket, and presses the button for the elevator.

Amaryllis reaches out and squeezes my arm as I step into the elevator with Stellen and his offerings.

"There'll be hot cocoa and fresh snickerdoodles waiting for you."

As the doors slide closed, I appreciate her not saying "have fun." Visiting gravesites isn't that sort of activity. The little squirrel in Stellen's hand looks at me knowingly. I can almost swear I see his nose twitch.

We load into my Jeep and drive in silence to the cemetery.

The groundskeeper is busy plowing snow from the walkways with his compact ride-on mower fitted with a snowplow attachment.

We wait patiently for him to notice us and turn off the engine.

He hops from the small vehicle and offers us that flat smile and head nod I remember seeing a thousand times. Death is an uncomfortable subject. Even for a man who literally makes his living caring for the deceased, the topic is one he still approaches carefully.

Smiling, I step forward. "Hello. We're looking for Stan and Crystal Jablonski?"

A dark shadow passes over his face and he tilts his head toward Stellen.

It's a small town. Everyone knows the sad story of his mother's losing battle with cancer, and his father's senseless murder. He turns and points to a small stand of leafless birch near the base of a hill. "Head straight toward those trees, take a left, and their plots are about halfway down, right after the black granite bench."

"Thank you."

Stellen follows me silently.

As we approach the black granite bench, the name Lindy McElroy gleams up from its surface. "Beloved mother and wife."

What will my headstone say? The moment I'm about to disappear into one of my mind movies, a sharp stab of sorrow shoots off Stellen like static electricity in the dark. Right, better get back to my big-sister duties. "Hey, I'm going to walk up the hill and visit Isadora's headstone and give you some privacy. Sound good?"

He's working so hard to hold back his emotions, he can barely nod his head.

Slipping away, I follow my detailed psychic memory back up the hill to the beautiful headstone for Myrtle Isadora Johnson Linder Duncan Willamet Rogers.

The delicate cardinal I purchased from the statuary in Broken Rock perches atop the headstone with the grace of a living creature. If not for the sprinkling of snow on his back and its dark granite color, I could almost make myself believe he's about to take flight.

Sadly, the bouquet of flowers in the small vase next to the massive slab of granite holds nothing more than shriveled floral remains.

It would appear Odell has abandoned his frequent cemetery visits now that he's in the ghost club.

Part of me is inexplicably sad about this development. There was something so touching about his steadfast care for my grandmother's plot. Although, I'm hardly one to talk. I've lived in Pin Cherry for over three years, and I've only been here once—twice counting today. It's awfully difficult to remember that someone is dead, and worry about a piece of stone and some grass, when you see them and feel their love every day. Of all the things that I discovered when I came to Pin Cherry, I think the existence of Ghost-ma is the most precious to me.

Reaching out, I brush snow from the little cardinal's back and kneel in front of the headstone. My finger traces the letters etched into the polished surface. I whisper each name quietly when I finish. If I'd hoped for some otherworldly experience, it does not arrive.

As I stare at the headstone and the decaying flora, my mind wanders into an Ebenezer Scrooge ghost of Christmas future scenario.

Who will visit my grave? Have I left an impression on this world? Are my philanthropic foundation and my monetary gifts to the community enough?

A soft tapping on my shoulder sends me leaping into the air like a cat who saw a cucumber—or is it a zucchini?

"Sorry, Mitzy, I didn't mean to scare you."

"It's all right. I was—"

Stellen presses his lips together, and my gaze takes in his red eyes and ragged breathing.

"Yeah, we don't have to talk about it. Let's go get some of that hot chocolate Amaryllis promised us."

He struggles to swallow and nods. I put my arm around his shoulders and try to absorb some of his pain as we make our way back to the Jeep.

His relationship with his father may have been rocky at best, but I know firsthand the pain of missing a loving mother who didn't get enough time on this planet.

CHAPTER 3

AFTER POWERING THROUGH two steaming mugs of cocoa and more snickerdoodles than anyone should count, I head back to the bookstore. My volunteer employee, and Isadora's best friend in life, is scanning over today's to-do list when I approach the back room.

"Hey, Twiggy. Anything I can do to help?"

She gets to her feet, tromps across the floor in her unmistakable biker boots, and stares at me without a word. Silently, she turns the punch list toward me. Twiggy is the only one who "knows I know."

My eyes widen in mock horror. It's the longest one yet. Grams is going straight-up ghost crazy planning this birthday extravaganza.

Before I can react, Pyewacket head butts me

and drops a stuffed rabbit from the children's section at my feet. His tail flicks impatiently as I bend to retrieve the item.

"Hey, buddy. I don't have time to play. Isadora is mad with power, and I need to help out." I leave the plush bunny on the floor.

"Reeeee-ow." A warning.

"Easy, Mr. Cuddlekins. We're friends. Remember?" Crouching, I pick up the rabbit and sigh. "If it's that important to you, I'll make a note of it."

This response seems to please him. He stalks out of the room without a backward glance.

Twiggy blows a raspberry. "Perfect. I've got this ridiculous list, and a crabby kitten. This day is really lookin' up, kid."

Shrugging helplessly, I offer the only help I can. "How about I walk over to the bank and get the drawer money for you?"

Getting the cash for the daily register operations in the bookstore has always been Twiggy's job. In fact, it was the hot topic of debate one of the first times she put me in my place. I was acting quite superior, and throwing around my heiress status, when she bluntly reminded me I know next to nothing about running a bookstore. Ever since, I've learned to respect the severe grey pixie cut and the wealth of information that comes along with it.

"That'd be great, doll. As you can see, I'm full up."

"Copy that."

As I turn to leave the back room, I trip over my own foot. Stumbling forward, I catch myself on the doorjamb and bang my head lightly. When I stand up, groaning and pressing a hand to my forehead, an all-too-familiar cackle resounds behind me.

"Thanks, kid. I needed that today."

And that, ladies and gentlemen, is why she works for free. She just wants to have front row seats to Mitzy's Believe It or Not Klutz Show.

Rather than head up to my swanky apartment and get pulled into an inevitable wardrobe debate with Grams, I skip out the side door and head down Main Street to the bank. I appreciate all the couture she collected for me, but I'll take my skinny jeans and a tee any day of the week.

The same number of boarded-up windows and long-vanished businesses exist as the first day I set foot in this town. However, now that I know the residents and call this place home, those little eyesores disappear into the background. The bustling diner, Rex's drugstore, and, of course, the sheriff's station take center stage.

Main Street looks lively, and well-kept. In fact, someone painted the windows of the bank with elaborate spring and Easter decorations. It must be a hobby of Tilly's—Tally's sister—because their brother's veterinary clinic and Myrtle's Diner sport similarly themed decor.

Quick backstory on the Sikanen family: Tally works at the diner. Tilly works at the bank. They're sisters. Their parents named each of their children after the town where he or she was conceived. The oldest sister in Tillamook, Wisconsin—Tilly; the youngest, in Tallahassee, Florida—Tally; and the middle child, the veterinarian brother, in Toledo, Ohio—Doc Ledo.

There are more employees in the bank than I would've expected, but the mood is cheery, and Tilly offers me a friendly wave as I enter.

The only hint of similarity between her and her sister is the welcoming smile. Where Tally sports a flame-red dye job and a tight bun, Tilly has let herself go mostly grey, or grey-blonde. She keeps her hair short, heavily backcombed and hair sprayed within an inch of its life.

Tally hustles around the diner in comfortable grease-resistant-soled shoes, slinging coffee and french fries with remarkable expertise.

Tilly walks with the grace of a finishing school graduate, and I've never seen her in anything besides kitten heels.

There's only one customer in line.

Hopping in line behind the other customer, I'm

mesmerized by the blue-black sheen of her hair. Thanks to some handy tips from the ghost of the fashion diva who lives in my bookstore, I can tell this perfectly bobbed hair is of the synthetic variety. The elaborately dressed woman in front of me is wearing a wig. No judgment. I rely on them heavily in my undercover work.

My mind wanders back to previous cases and, without warning—

BANG!

What the—

"Everyone on the ground. This is a robbery. My friends and I are only here for the money. You cooperate, you don't get hurt."

It surprises me to discover that I'm already on the ground. I don't remember how I got there, but the sudden shock of a shotgun blast to the ceiling probably had something to do with it. Ballsy move by the masked gunmen! The bank is across the street from the sheriff's station and barely half a block down. Even the distracted Deputy Furious Monkeys might hear a gunshot.

"Follow those rules! Nobody gets hurt."

Blerg. The entire time the guy in the rabbit mask was talking, I got lost in the world inside my head. Now that I've regained an awareness of the outside world, it's time to admire the clever disguises worn by the bank robbers. The rabbit-masked guy, Wonderland timekeeper the White Rabbit, complete with large ears, stands on top of Tilly's desk. I can't see her, but I hope she's safely on the floor somewhere behind him. And yes, somehow Pye knew there would be a rabbit in my day. I'll be sure to give him credit when I get out of here.

The tall, unkempt, and crazy Mad Hatter guards the front entrance with the shotgun that surely put the hole in the ceiling. And the woman who used to be standing in front of me turns out to be a Queen of Hearts look-alike, and is hard at work stuffing cash from the teller drawers into a knockoff Gucci backpack.

They can't be very good bank robbers if they can't even afford a real Gucci. Am I right, Grams? Unfortunately, my paranormal sidekick is tethered to the bookshop and will be of no use in my current situation. However, just when I thought things couldn't get any more interesting, I'm rewarded with the blockbuster movie-trailer entrance of Alice and the Cheshire Cat! Her standard blue dress and white apron are paired with opera-length white gloves, harlequin tights, and black Doc Martens, while the Cat's wardrobe combines a plushy head with tight black jeans and a black-and-purple striped leather coat. Fantastic. The gang's all here!

Now, to get down to the business of figuring a way out of this mess. Think. Think. Think.

"I said down on the ground!"

Oops. During my intense brainstorming sesh, I seem to have stood up. Before I can hustle myself back down to the chilly granite floor, some helpful bank employee calls out, "You can't threaten her. She's the sheriff's girlfriend."

It doesn't take a psychic to figure out how that information is going to be used.

The White Rabbit hops from the desk—no pun intended—and stalks toward me. If not for the cartoonish mask covering his face, I'm sure I'd be treated to an annoying sneer.

"Well, well, well. Did you hear that, friends? We've got ourselves a top-notch hostage. This here is the sheriff's best girl."

The Mad Hatter snickers as he drops the blinds on the front windows and peers between the slats.

"How's the take lookin', Queenie?" the White Rabbit calls.

The individual in the Queen of Hearts disguise sports a high Victorian collar and red-and-gold corset. From this distance, I can't be sure if it's a woman or a— Hold on! What's the point of psychic powers if I can't use them to clarify some information? Reaching out with my special abilities, I confirm that the person in the Queen of Hearts regalia is a tall, slender man. But the Alice character is definitely a woman.

The Queen of Hearts holds up her imitation designer backpack and shakes her head. "Not enough to pay for the tea party, Ears."

Oh brother. I love a good cover story as much as the next guy, but let's not beat a dead horse.

The White Rabbit hooks an arm around me and brandishes his pistol as he shouts, "Who runs this joint?"

A man whom I have to assume is the bank manager, because I've never met him, gets to his feet and waves a hand as though he's back in high school homeroom and the teacher is taking roll.

The White Rabbit lifts his chin in recognition. "You're gonna have to open the vault, pal."

The comfortably round, balding man inches forward. In the movie version of this scene, the director would've already established that the man is days from retirement. I allow the classic trope to infiltrate this real-world disaster.

"Um, you'll have to excuse me—Mr.—um, Rabbit. Our vault . . . no money. Um, only safe deposit boxes." The poor man is shaking and stuttering like a teenager giving a reproductive-cycle presentation in health class.

"What's that, old man? You trying to tell me you got no money in your vault?"

The Mad Hatter calls from the window, "Ears,

we gotta hit it. There's some action over at the pig farm."

Despite the gun waving near my person, I nod in acknowledgment of the clever reference to the Pin Cherry sheriff's station. My action does not go unnoticed.

"You think your boyfriend is gonna come and save you? I got news for you, doll face. You're our ticket out of this one-horse town."

They say fortune favors the bold. "Well, if you were planning on using that ticket, I'd say the bus left thirty seconds ago."

The White Rabbit shoves the gun under my chin and growls into my ear. "I might look like a cuddly storybook character, but I can assure you I'm not joking. You cooperate, or you die."

Looks like I'm officially down the rabbit hole now! "Understood." I mumble my response carefully, to avoid irritating the criminal or activating his itchy trigger finger. My cooperation is rewarded with the removal of the firearm from my jawline.

He aims the gun at the bank manager and offers him a fresh threat. "Either you open that vault, or I shoot you. Seems like a pretty simple choice."

I'd have to agree with that heist logic.

The bank manager struggles to swallow, presses a hand to his chest, and staggers toward the vault.

The Queen of Hearts has finished raiding the

drawers, and vaults back over the counter. As the man in glam attire approaches, the teller calls out a warning from behind the counter. "Mr. Curb has a bad heart. Please don't hurt him."

The White Rabbit turns to offer her some two-bit threat, but Hatter interrupts his flow. "They're on the move, Ears. It's now or never."

The furry criminal presses the gun into the middle of Mr. Curb's back, and the bank manager shuffles forward in fear.

When he reaches the massive steel door, he removes a heavy key ring from his coat pocket, and his hand shakes violently as he attempts to open the door.

"Mr. Curb? I'm Mitzy Moon. Would you like me to open the door for you?"

The terrified man turns to look at me while Mr. Rabbit struggles to pick a target for his weapon. "Hey, doll face, I call the shots."

"Absolutely. It just seems like you're in a bit of a hurry, and I think I can operate that key a little faster than Mr. Curb. But it's up to you." My bravado is as false as false can be. Inside, I'm scared for the safety of all the hostages. If the movies have taught me anything, the money's insured. It's the loss of life that's irreplaceable.

"Hand her the keys, Curb."

Mr. Curb's tremulous hand nearly drops the

keys before I get hold of them. The White Rabbit shoves me toward the door, and I slip the key into the lock.

The terrified bank manager sweats profusely as he offers me a tip. "You have to turn it several times, dear."

That reminds me of the hefty brass key that opens my bookshop. Its unique triangle barrel must be turned three times to activate the tumblers hidden within the intricately carved wooden door.

There's an audible click within this thick metal door, and Mr. Rabbit pushes me out of the way. He grips the large circular handle and twists it counter-clockwise.

Interesting. He knows his way around a vault, which means this probably isn't his first robbery. Plus, he's taking quite a chance sticking around after his lookout warned him of law enforcement on the move. Maybe he doesn't rob banks for the money. Maybe he robs them for the thrill of the chase.

The massive steel door creaks open and reveals a single wooden table in a well-lit interior. The table is empty. Three visible walls are nothing more than row upon row of safe deposit boxes.

The White Rabbit turns to face Mr. Curb and I imagine his whiskers twitch as he raises his gun. "Where's the cash?"

"Well, like I said, this is only—"

The White Rabbit lunges forward and presses the gun to Mr. Curb's chest. "Don't waste your breath. Where's the cash?"

The color drains from the bank manager's face, and it looks as though he could drop any minute. Mr. Curb points down, as though he's indicating Satan's domain, and whispers in a frightened tone. "In the old vault."

The White Rabbit shouts over our heads. "Alice, Smiley, you're with me. Queenie, watch the back door."

The Queen of Hearts hustles toward the back door, but calls out, "What's going on?"

"There's another vault in the basement."

An update from Mr. Rabbit's front-window lookout. "Hope that hostage is worth it, Ears. It's not looking good out there."

"Calm down, Hatter. We've got a free ride on the Reading."

If I get his reference correctly, he thinks I'm his ticket to take a lap around the Monopoly board, penalty free. I've got some news for this poor misplaced storybook character: Sheriff Erick Harper doesn't play favorites. He won't let criminals walk free, just to save my hide.

The White Rabbit keeps his gun trained on me

while Alice and the Cheshire Cat lead the way downstairs.

The vault in the basement is . . . older. Darker. And, dare I say, sinister?

"You got the keys, doll face. Open it up."

He releases his hold on me, but keeps the gun trained squarely at my back as I move toward the locking mechanism. The antique mood ring on my left hand sizzles to life, and at the same moment my clairaudience reveals whispers within the walls.

Yeesh. This is how every horror movie I've ever seen starts. Some hapless coed ignores the warning signs and—

"Hustle up, doll face. The fuzz is breathing down our necks."

I want to focus. I need to focus, but when he talks about law enforcement breathing down his neck—you guessed it—images of Erick Harper's hot, inviting breath on my neck distract me.

"Now!"

Right. I fumble with the key ring and grab the only other key that looks old enough to belong to this vault. As I insert it into the lock. *Twist. Twist. Clunk.* And is that a hiss? The whispering grows louder.

The White Rabbit grabs my shoulder and pulls me back as the Cheshire Cat and Alice open the vault.

I wish I could report that my psychic senses were glitching. But when the ghostly form of a ski-mask-covered face oozes out of the barely open vault, the White Rabbit and his gun suddenly become the least of my worries.

CHAPTER 4 - ERICK

"PAULSEN, I want you to get a sniper on the roof of Rex's, and send two deputies down the alley behind the bank." The flaps on my ridiculous deerstalker hat are interfering with my peripheral. Time to sacrifice warmth for visibility. I yank the cap off my head and throw it into the vehicle.

"That's a 10-4 on the deputies in the alley, Sheriff. But we don't have a sniper. You're the best shot on the force."

Not to toot my own horn, but Deputy Paulsen is correct. "What's the ETA on the reinforcements from Broken Rock?"

"They're five minutes out."

"10-4. When Boomer gets here, send him up. He's a better shot than me any day of the week."

Paulsen's grim expression seems to show disagreement, but she always keeps it professional. She widens her stance and nods her head. "10-4."

"Johnson, take a position east. Stay sharp." He's one of my youngest guys. I can't risk putting him too close to the action. I don't plan on losing anyone today.

Johnson jogs in the direction I pointed, tightening the strap on his Kevlar vest as he goes. I don't know what we're dealing with, but Deputy Baird said she heard a gunshot, and somebody at that bank triggered the silent alarm. Reaching into my strategically parked cruiser, I grab the bullhorn, stand behind the door, and make first contact. "This is Sheriff Harper. We have the bank surrounded. We're interested in negotiating the safe release of the hostages. Who do I have the pleasure of negotiating with?"

No response.

There's a quick bend in one of the slats of the blinds behind an Easter basket filled with brightly painted eggs. I wish Mitzy could see this scene. I know how much she enjoys great imagery. Something tells me she'd get a kick out of a bank robbery decorated for spring. Pressing the microphone clipped to my shoulder, I check in with my deputies and make sure everyone's in position.

Paulsen and I have secured Main Street, and sent all the looky-loos indoors. Gilbert has the west and Johnson has the east. Baird and the new guy headed down the alley. I'd feel better if we had that sniper in place, but it'll be a couple more minutes before that concern is addressed.

"Sheriff, we found the vehicle."

"You sure, Baird?"

"10-4. Ran the plates. Came up registered to a vehicle reported stolen down south two days ago."

"Get Clarence on the horn."

"10-4."

Now they'll have to negotiate with me whether they like it or not. In less than five minutes, their cleverly hidden getaway vehicle will be dangling from Clarence's big steel hook. "Dispatch. Patch me into the bank."

There are a series of clicks and a long pause, but eventually there's ringing.

And more ringing. A frustrating amount of ringing. Doesn't sound like anyone's going to answer. "Try another extension."

"10-4." Dispatch works her way through the roster at the bank. Finally, I'm rewarded with a soft whisper. "Pin Cherry Harbor Bank & Trust, how can I invest in your day?"

You have to hand it to Tilly. Even in the middle of a terrifying situation, she puts her best foot forward. "Tilly, it's Sheriff Harper."

"Oh, geez, Sheriff. It's awful. There are five of

them. With big guns. They've taken Mitzy hostage!"

The blood in my veins turns to ice, and I feel a sickening plunge in my gut. After two tours overseas, I figured a bank robbery is hardly something to get excited about. That changed the instant Tilly spoke *her* name. Knowing that the woman I love is messed up in this, and might have a gun pressed to her back, just raised the limit at the table. I hate to say, I'm not much of a gambler.

"Sheriff? Sheriff, what should we do?"

"Everyone needs to remain calm. We've got the situation under control out here. Once I get them on the phone, I'll find out what they want. You better hang up now, Tilly. I don't want you putting yourself in any danger."

"I don't know about danger, Sheriff. They all went down to the basement, to the old vault. Anyway, there's only the one boy up here at the front window, and a sweet young girl at the back door."

Classic small-town gossip. Bless her heart for giving me every single piece of information I could've wanted. Before I can thank her properly, there's a terrified squeak, and an angry voice shouting something about killing hostages.

The phone hits something with a thud, but we aren't disconnected.

"Look, lady, I said everybody on the floor. Get over there in front of the counter with the others."

An uncomfortable silence.

"Nobody moves. Got it?"

My teeth feel like they could crack as I clench my jaw and listen intently. I heard at least four voices offer their agreement.

"Everybody drop your cell phones in here. Now!"

Thud. Clack. Clack. Clack.

Four phones drop into something, maybe a trashcan.

Lights and sirens rip onto the end of Main Street, and Johnson signals the cars to halt.

Boomer leaps out of his vehicle, helmet in one hand, long-range sniper rifle in the other. His dark brown eyes glint with excitement as he crouches low and jogs up the sidewalk.

"Harper."

"Good to see you, Boomer. I need you on the roof. ASAP."

"10-4. How many unfriendlies?"

"Five. Unconfirmed."

"Hostages?"

"Four in the main room. At least one more in the basement vault. Also unconfirmed."

"Do I have the green light?"

"Negative. On my order only."

"Come on, Harper. You're takin' all the fun out of it."

Doesn't seem like the most professional thing to tell him, but Boomer and I go way back. "Nothing fun about it. My girlfriend is in there. So, on my order, and that's final."

"Understood, bro. I'll let you know when I'm in position."

The cool wind has nearly disappeared. This morning Boomer would've had to factor in twenty-eight to thirty mile-per-hour crosswinds. Now—I lick my finger and hold it up—it's dropped to under three.

I need to get someone talking. The key to any good negotiation is establishing rapport with the leader. The putz who threatened Tilly and left the phone off the hook can't possibly be the mastermind behind this heist.

Paulsen paces beside her cruiser like a tank on maneuvers. Her mother is a teller at the bank, but if that's causing her any worry, she's keeping it on lockdown.

The thing I can't figure out is what led them to the vault in the basement. That was abandoned fifty years ago after a security guard and a masked gunman killed each other in a robbery gone wrong.

I wasn't around back then—I wasn't even a twinkle in my mother's eye—but when you work law-enforcement in a small town, there are certain stories folks never forget. Point being, there's no money in that vault. As far as I know, they house the weekly cash delivery in a relatively compact safe hidden behind a false wall in the manager's office. I wish I knew what took them to the basement.

"I'm in position, Sheriff."

"10-4, Boomer. Anything to report?"

"Yeah, it's colder than a witch's—"

"Not on this frequency. Let's keep it professional out there."

Deputy Johnson and the new guy both offer confirmation of message received. As for the rest of the deputies, it's easy to imagine them snickering into their gloves.

The last car of reinforcements arrives from Broken Rock. Paulsen sends them into the sheriff's station to man the phones and stay warm. There's no telling how long this standoff will last, and we'll need reinforcements with unfrozen trigger fingers if we hope to keep our advantage.

CHAPTER 5

INSIDE MY LITTLE PSYCHIC HEAD, there are at least five emotions swirling around, struggling to get the upper hand. The ghost of a former bank robber slipped out of the basement vault. Based on reactions, I'm pretty confident in saying I'm the only one who can see the thing. However, I have no interest in letting this sketchy ghost find out that he's been seen. I cough and let my gaze dart to the floor.

"You see the cash, Smiley?"

The Cheshire Cat and Alice peer into the dark cavern, pop a light on from one of their phones, and grumble loudly. "Nothing, Ears. That guy sent us on a wild-goose chase!" The two co-conspirators complete their search of the ten-foot by fifteen-foot space, and exit in a huff.

My furry white captor loosens his hold on me

and turns all of his attention toward the fragile, fumbling bank manager. The only thing is, when I focus on Mr. Curb, I'm not getting any fear. I'm picking up on some subtle self-satisfied vibes and a hint of anticipation. Did he know about the haunted vault?

As if on cue, the lights in the hallway flicker, and an icy blast of air fills the space.

The three heist buddies exchange nervous glances. Alice says what they're all thinking, "Hey, like, what's up with the lights? And am I trippin' or did it get, like, mega cold?"

Both men nod, and the White Rabbit aims his handgun at Mr. Curb. "What's the big idea? There's no money in there. Why'd you bring us down to this Halloween freak show? Did you think we'd be scared?"

Mr. Curb returns to his fumbling and stuttering, but I'm picking up the truth beneath the bunny's words. The White Rabbit is scared, and so are his friends.

It doesn't seem like Mr. Curb can see the ghost, but it would appear that he's a firm believer in the paranormal. Perhaps he's heard stories, or had previous run-ins with the otherworldly resident of his bank. Now that I know his fragility is an act, I plan to help him use it to our advantage.

He stutters out a confused response, and the bank robbers are getting restless.

Time for some "more flies with honey," as Grams always says. "Hey, Ears. Can I call you Ears?"

He spins on his blue canvas high-tops and turns the gun sideways like every gangster in every movie you've ever seen. "You got something to say, blondie?"

"I appreciate all the effort you're putting into nicknames. Believe me, I do. My name isn't Blondie, or Doll Face. It's Mitzy. And the longer you guys hang out in this bank, the more time you're giving law enforcement to put their snipers in place."

Definite spike in the fear vibe coming from Alice. Perfect.

"You already know the sheriff and I are involved. Why not use that to your advantage, now, before things get out of hand or one of your partners gets nervous and takes this simple armed robbery to a whole new level?" I hope he picks up on what I'm implying, which is the danger of a restless crew and a room full of frightened hostages.

He's smarter than his cuddly mask looks. "We got a van out back. I don't need your help."

They say timing is everything . . .

The Queen of Hearts appears at the top of the

stairs with some bad news. "Ears, they're towing the van!"

It's tough to keep the grin from my lips. "You were saying?"

He grips the back of my neck and presses the gun hard into my chest. "How did you know?"

The truth is, I didn't know, but if I can somehow get him to believe that I'm able to predict — "You know how it is. When you've been dating someone for a while, you kinda get how their mind works."

Despite my elevated heart rate and shallow breathing, my bluff seems to float.

"Get back to the door, Queenie. Keep me posted. Blondie here—"

"Mitzy."

"Yeah, whatever. This one's got some ideas."

Mr. Curb breathes a sigh of relief, and the White Rabbit insists the manager lead us all back to the main room.

Trying to gather as much information as possible on my return trip, I let my eyes scan every inch of the bank as it flows past. Something might come in useful for psychic replay later. The first thing I notice in the main room is that all the hostages have been grouped together by the counter, and Tilly has a decidedly smug expression on her face. When I catch her eye, she winks and nods subtly towards her desk.

Fortunately, my extra abilities snatch the word *phone* from the air, and when I scan the desktop, I note the missing receiver. Someone's listening. Hopefully, it's someone who matters.

The White Rabbit drags me toward the front windows and peeks out. "What the heck, Hatter? You didn't tell me they set up blockades."

"I told you they were on the move."

The White Rabbit shakes his head, and I sense his anger rising. "On the move is a little different than in position." He pushes me into a seat and lazily aims his gun. "So what's the sheriff's next move?"

I need to test this relationship. I wait to see if he'll offer my name.

His mask bobs left and right. "Mitzy. What's his next move?"

Success. At some point, I may try to reach out with my psychic senses, but for now, I need to get one of these people out of here. "He's going to want to know your demands. If you want to get the upper hand, release a hostage before he asks for one. Then you'll have more negotiating power."

The White Rabbit's ears shake back and forth, and I can tell he's struggling with my recommendation. As 'he should be. My recommendation makes absolutely no sense. But my goal isn't to give him the upper hand, my goal is to get these hostages out one at a time.

He glances toward the row of hostages and back to the bank manager currently held at gunpoint by the one he calls Smiley.

"Bank manager or the old lady?"

Leaning forward, I lower my voice to a whisper. "Between you and me, the sheriff is a bit of a mama's boy. I think the old lady will get you more juice."

I'll apologize to Erick later for the slander on his person, but I really want to get Tilly out of this bank.

"You, in the pink."

Tilly presses a hand to her chest and looks from me to the ringleader. "Me? My name's Tilly Sikanen."

"Tilly, get over here."

"Oh, right away." She struggles to maintain her modesty and get to her feet in a skirt suit, but eventually manages the task. As she approaches, I can feel the air thicken with her fear. "How can I help you, sir?"

He points to the door, and that's the moment I realize I'm still holding the ring of keys.

"Hatter, cut the zip tie. Mitzy has the keys. We'll lock it proper after we let this one out."

Surprisingly, Hatter does as he's told without protest. He's absolutely *not* the brains of the operation.

"You're letting me out? Why thank you, son. My sciatica was bothering me something terrible on the cold floor, but I didn't want to complain."

The White Rabbit puts his hand on the door, and I step forward. He turns and aims the gun at me. "Don't get any bright ideas. She's the only one going out."

"Understood. But we haven't communicated that we're letting out a hostage. If you open that door, they might start firing. Is it all right if I call the sheriff?" Pulling my cell from my back pocket, I offer it up innocently.

Mr. Rabbit turns on his cohort. "You didn't take their phones?"

Hatter waves his gun dangerously toward the row of hostages. "I did. I did, mostly. She was with you. You should've taken it."

I'm not against internal strife. I just want it to kick in after Tilly is safely outside. "Look, guys. It's nothing to fight about. I didn't make any calls. And I'm asking permission to place a call that will help you out. You don't want anybody on your team to get shot, do ya Ears?" I'll try using the more familiar form of his name bandied about by his fellow robbers.

It catches him off guard, and he nods toward the phone. "Make it quick. Just tell him I'm releasing a hostage; don't try to give him any coded information."

"Copy that."

The Mad Hatter's head turns toward me when I speak the phrase. Perhaps he's had some experience on a movie set. Perhaps it's coincidence. A random clue that may or may not prove useful. I'll worry about that once they've released Tilly.

I hit speed dial and the call rings.

"Put it on speakerphone."

I tap the icon and comply, as a tense but familiar voice comes through. "This is Sheriff Harper. Who am I speaking with?"

Seems like Erick and I are more of a similar mind than I guessed. "Hey, Erick. It's Mitzy. We just wanted to call and let you know that they're going to release one of the hostages. So don't shoot, all right?"

Part of me hears him breathe a sigh of relief and part of me feels the rush of concern that floats through his body. Seems like I won't have to work as hard as I thought to hook up the psychic link. "We're sending out Tilly. The Mad Hatter's gonna open the door, and the White Rabbit has a gun trained on me. So definitely tell your men to stand down."

"10-4. Are you pulling my leg with these names, Moon?"

"No, sir. The Wonderland gang's all here."

The White Rabbit waves the gun at me. "That's enough."

The door opens, and I gently propel Tilly forward. She covers her eyes against the sharp light of the midday sun.

A series of commands echo through the phone as they flow over the radio, and rapid footfalls approach the door.

Ears shouts, "Shut the damn door, Hatter!"

Erick confirms. "We've got her."

I'm about to respond, but Mr. Rabbit grabs my phone and ends the call. "Lock the door, *Mitzy*."

CHAPTER 6

ONE DOWN, FOUR TO GO. Five if I count myself,
but I honestly don't see that in the cards. At least
Tilly is safe. I'll have to use everything Silas ever
taught me to get inside the heads of these robbers.
As I twist the key in the lock, my temporary connec-
tion with Erick vanishes. Maybe it was never there.
It was probably wishful thinking. Regardless, I need
to step up my game and figure out how to get the
next hostage out.

"I'll be taking those." The leader of the gang offers his gloved palm, and I drop the key ring onto it.
He tosses it in the pocket of his fancy orange waistcoat. And not for the first time, I have to admire the
detail and authenticity of the wardrobe. Whoever
chose the disguises and took on costume design has

a flare. Was it the Queen of Hearts? Possibly. The man in glam definitely has the most style.

"I know you didn't ask, Mr. Rabbit, but you need to come up with your list of demands. If you wait until the sheriff asks for it, you'll look like an amateur. Don't make a long list. Don't make it a bunch of insane things. Figure out what you need to get out of here safely, ask for it, and offer a hostage in exchange for each line item."

The fuzzy-ear-topped mask tilts. "Seems like you might've done this before. You weren't planning on robbing this place today, were you?"

Time to reveal something and hopefully build trust. "Funny you should mention it. I guess it runs in my blood. My dad did fifteen in the state pen for armed robbery. Personally, I'm not much more than a petty thief, but I know what it looks like getting caught." No need to tell him I didn't know my father was even alive when he committed that robbery and did his stint in Clearwater.

"Whoa. Your dad's hard core. Smiley got popped for boosting a car when he was a minor, but his dad greased a few palms and got him off with some community service."

My plan is working. "Nice. I dated a guy who paid his way through school boosting cars. I know a thing or two about hot wiring. Which brings me back to your list. You need a getaway vehicle. And you need it soon."

The Mad Hatter pipes up behind us. "Hey, looks like shift change."

The White Rabbit leans toward the window to peek out, and I join him. He doesn't yell at me, which is progress.

One by one, Erick is calling in officers and sending out replacements. The new team is wearing a different uniform, probably from Broken Rock. They have far more officers on staff and generally back us up during large community events or situations like this.

Mr. Rabbit looks at the Mad Hatter and shakes his head. "Those guys look like SWAT."

No need for me to soothe his nerves. Let them think it's SWAT. It will motivate them to get moving on this negotiation.

"Maybe we'll just ask 'em to give us our van back." He moves away from the window and reaches under his mask to scratch his face.

"Possibly, but that van isn't gonna carry enough velocity to break through barricades. You need a bus. With a full tank of gas and curtains over all the windows."

The White Rabbit's masked face nods in appreciation. "Solid plan, blondie."

I let the comment lie and gesture toward a desk on the opposite side of the room from Tilly's.

If there's any chance that someone is still listening on that open line, I don't want to draw any attention to it. "I'll start making a list. They'll need some time to get the bus kitted out. Let's ask for food in exchange for a hostage to get the ball rolling."

The White Rabbit follows me to the desk, flops onto a rolly office chair and kicks his feet up as though he hasn't a care in the world. "Yeah, put that all down."

As I'm codifying the requests, the mood ring on my left hand turns to ice, and the hairs on the back of my neck stand on end.

Without warning, a stack of deposit slips flies off the center island and flutters to the floor like feathers in the wind.

The previously calm leader is on his feet in a second, aiming his gun into empty air. The masked ghost of yesteryear is enjoying a hearty laugh. I force my gaze to wander around the room as though I don't see him, but his wild polyester button down with its enormous collar and the high-waisted bell-bottom pants reveal a clue about his origin. Whoever this man is, it would appear he attempted to rob the bank in the 1970s. The shiny shirt is unbuttoned nearly to his ethereal naval, and there's a gaudy gold chain dangling from his otherworldly neck.

"Right on, sister. You like what you see?" He leers in my general direction.

Oops, I may have stared at a specific location for a tick too long. Better cover up fast. "What was that? Is there a door open?"

Mr. Rabbit jogs to the hallway and calls out. "Queenie, did you open the back door?"

"No. But I think I heard footsteps on the roof."

The inexplicable localized tornado is immediately forgotten. The White Rabbit extends the phone. "Call your sweetheart and tell him to pull back, or I shoot a hostage."

Taking the phone, I nod furiously. "Understood. And if he pulls back, let's send out the security guard in exchange."

Mr. Rabbit looks toward the lineup of hostages and leans back. "Security guard? The whole reason we targeted this joint is because they don't have a security guard. You feeling all right, doll face?"

My throat tightens and my stomach clinches with fear. The security guard seated at the end of the row of hostages isn't human.

There's a second ghost! And if he or his masked counterpart overheard, I may have tipped my hand. Time to lean into every blonde joke I've ever heard. "Whoops, I guess my roots are showing. It's a bank.

I just assumed there was a security guard. I thought that'd be the person you'd want to get rid of, you know? Never mind! When the cops pull back, we can send out the teller. She looks like she's about to faint. The last thing you need is a medical emergency on your hands. Then you'd have to let a doctor in, and who knows how that would turn out." I'm rambling and spitballing simultaneously. Never one of my best strategies. I'm eager to put as much dialogue distance as possible between my slip of the tongue and the next decision.

"Yeah, call your guy."

Putting the phone on speaker without being asked will hopefully gain me some additional brownie points.

"Sheriff Harper here."

"Hey, Sheriff. They're working on their list of demands. In the meantime, if you're willing to send some food over, they'll release another hostage."

"10-4. Myrtle's Diner?"

"That would be great. We've got five hostages, including me, and five *others*."

The White Rabbit smacks the phone from my hand and raises his gun. "I said no tricks. Remember? Don't be giving away information."

"Sorry! I was only thinking about a headcount for food. Honestly, I didn't mean anything by it." Now seems like the wrong time to tell him how they would already have that information from the hostage debrief with Tilly.

He sniffs sharply and rubs his free hand against his throat.

I hear opportunity knocking. "Are you guys thirsty? Should I have them send over some drinks?"

While he ponders that question, I retrieve the phone and discover the call didn't get dropped when the cell hit the floor. "Are you still there, Sheriff?"

"10-4."

His response is curt and to the point, but every one of my special abilities picks up on the tension, fear, and helplessness bubbling beneath the surface.

"Can you send over a few sodas and a few ice teas too?" I glance toward the hostages and shrug. Two of them nod their heads.

"Give us twenty, okay? We'll send someone in with the food."

Mr. Rabbit steps toward me, shaking his head and pointing his gun toward the roof.

"That's no good, Sheriff. We need you to pull your men off the roof immediately. Show us some good faith. When the food is ready, just have somebody drop it outside the door, and I'll pick it up—" I glance at the White Rabbit and tilt my head back and forth in a nonverbal request to proceed.

He nods.

"Yeah, I'll grab the food and we'll release a hostage. Deal?"

Erick's tone lightens, and I sense he's pleased with the way I'm running the negotiation. "We'll get the order placed, Moon. You be sure to—"

The White Rabbit grabs the phone, ends the call, and shoves my mobile into the pocket of his coat.

I hope that ring of keys in there doesn't scratch the screen. It's a weird thing to think about in a time of crisis, but I've never owned a legit new phone until now. I was really trying to take good care of it.

A typewriter crashes to the floor behind us, and the Mad Hatter fires his shotgun.

Less than a second later, a voice booms over the bullhorn. "You have ten seconds to let me know everyone's all right in there. If I don't hear from Mitzy, we're coming in!"

Shockingly, Mr. Rabbit seems to be frozen.

No time to waste. "Mr. Rabbit, I'm going to take my phone out of your pocket. I gotta call the sheriff or they'll come busting in with concussion grenades and who knows what else." I have no idea what the procedure is, but I need to use a word that sounds scary. I put my left hand in the air as I reach into his jacket pocket with my right. His gaze is locked onto the broken typewriter on the floor.

The call barely rings once. "Mitzy?"

Gone are the professional voice and the "Sheriff Harper" introduction. Erick is worried, and it shows.

"I'm here. Everyone's fine. A typewriter fell off one of the desks and the Mad Hatter overreacted. No one's hurt. You get your guys to back off and send the food. We're all right."

The White Rabbit snaps out of his daze, but the gun in his left hand hangs as limp as a wilting flower. "Just keep the phone, doll face."

I slip it into the pocket of my jeans and breathe a sigh of relief.

He shakes the gun toward the recent ruckus. "What's going on here? There's nobody over there. What made that typewriter—?"

When in doubt, lie it out. "You know how these old buildings are. The foundations are always shifting. Plus, they're drafty and unstable. A small town like this can't really afford to update their infrastructure. You saw how many buildings are boarded up on Main Street. I wouldn't worry about it. No one was hurt, that's the important thing."

While I soothe the ringleader's frayed nerves, the Mad Hatter approaches with his comically large head hanging. "I'm out, Ears."

"What?"

Hatter lowers his voice and leans toward the

leader. "I'm outta ammo. Normally, I fire one into the ceiling. Queenie grabs the cash and we go. I never had to fire a second shot or a third."

Mr. Rabbit reaches out and smacks the Mad Hatter upside the head. "You knucklehead! Don't let the hostages know. I'll see if Smiley has a backup."

The White Rabbit wanders off to check the Cheshire Cat's ammunition situation, and I stroll casually toward the hostages. I crouch at the end of the row, directly in front of the ghost of security guards past, and address the three remaining employees. "Is it true that you don't have a security guard?"

The ghost at the end of the row crosses his arms and sticks out his lower lip like a child being sent to timeout.

The teller answers. "Oh, you betcha. I know the whole story. There was a terrible robbery here when I was seven. Seems like a century ago, you know."

A century? I can't believe this woman's job involves math.

She tugs at her mousy brown bob and swallows audibly. "It was the talk of the town for decades, dontcha know. Folks were still jawing about it when my little Pauly was born."

This can't be happening. But there can't be that

many Paulys in Pin Cherry. Before my mouth can formulate the question, my special abilities deliver the answer. The teller is Deputy Pauly Paulsen's mother. Great, now I have guilt and I missed part of the story.

"Oh, there were a bunch of gunmen and a shootout, for sure. Some of our good citizens were murdered—our neighbor, Lindy McElroy among them. God rest her. Well, those robbers shot the security guard, and I think he even shot one of them. Anyway, that's when they stopped using the vault in the basement, and put the—"

I raise a hasty finger to my lips. Who knows exactly what she was going to say, but I could definitely sense she was about to give away a key piece of information about the missing cash. We definitely need to get her out of here. "Thanks for filling me in. When they deliver the food, we're going to send you out. All right?"

She gazes at me with grateful brown eyes that look nothing like her bully of a daughter's. "Honestly, dear? I'm getting out of here?"

The middle-aged man next to her stiffens. "I have a family. I should be the next one released."

My eyes seethe with contempt. "I suppose you would've been one of those men on the Titanic that shoved a pregnant woman aside to get into a lifeboat." I point firmly at the teller. "She leaves next. Any questions?"

He presses his lips into a thin line and shakes his head.

The ghostly guard looks up with a flicker of hope in his eyes.

At that moment, I take the risk—stare directly at him, and wink.

His shimmering mouth makes a perfect O and his eyes widen with a shade of hope they haven't seen in decades.

THE SOUND OF A GUNSHOT inside the bank really threw me off my game. Being on the outside, with Mitzy trapped on the inside, is wreaking havoc on my concentration. Squeezing the button on the side of my mic, I ask the relief team from Broken Rock to report. As the calls come in over the radio, I roll through the facts and my options.

My guys are safe inside the station, warming up and getting food.

Odell's packaging up the delivery for the bank. Paulsen wants to be the one to take it to the door. There's a gunman with an itchy trigger finger inside, and that means a simple food delivery is high risk. Seems like Paulsen has nerves of steel, though. And I'd rather accept a volunteer for the task than appoint a deputy to risk their life.

Thanks to the information we collected from Tilly and Mitzy's not-so-subtle hints, I know there are four hostages left. Wait, Mitzy said there were five hostages including her. I only heard four phones drop into the bin before Tilly came out. Maybe one of the remaining hostages is from an older generation and doesn't carry a cell phone.

Although, it could mean there's a child involved. My worst nightmare. I hate seeing kids in danger.

If I know Miss Moon, and I may know her too well, she's working every angle she can think of to keep the hostages safe and trick the bad guys into making a mistake.

The problem with Mitzy is that she's too willing to put herself in danger to accomplish her goals.

"Sheriff Harper, food is ready to go."

Odell's prior military training shows in every calculated movement. He's gotta be worried about his granddaughter, Mitzy, stuck in a bank with a bunch of armed robbers, but it doesn't show on his experienced face.

As he carries out a red milk crate filled with to-go bags and beverages, the sun shines on his silver buzz cut and he nods competently in my direction.

"Paulsen, you ready?"

"10-4, Sheriff. I take the delivery to the bank,

place it two feet to the right of the hinge, so they have to open the door wide and let Mitzy walk out in full view. Boomer's in position and he'll be ready to take a shot at your command."

"Okay, Paulsen. It's go time. No heroics. Deliver the food and get back to safety."

Despite her current campaign for sheriff in the election later this year, Paulsen is a loyal deputy and always puts the assignment first. She may be occasionally hotheaded and generally suspect the worst, but she's reliable and, in the end, fair.

Paulsen takes the crate from Odell, and he saunters toward me.

"How's Mitzy holdin' up?"

"She has things under control. She's my point of contact on the inside and she's making a list of their demands."

His ready chuckle lightens my burden. "If I didn't know better, Sheriff, I'd say she's the mastermind behind the heist."

It feels good to laugh, even if it's only for a minute. "I was thinking the same thing."

Odell leans in close and whispers for my ears only. "Anybody updated Myrtle Isadora?"

The mention of the ghost of Mitzy's grandmother always blows my mind. When Mitzy told me she could see ghosts, and the ghost of her grandmother was sort of alive and well in the bookshop, I had serious doubts about her sanity. However, once I witnessed Myrtle Isadora moving things around the bookstore and felt the chill envelop my body as she passed by, they made a believer out of me. "Wasn't anybody I could tell. Would you mind doing the honors?"

Odell nods once and heads down the street in his shirtsleeves. I'm not sure whether it's the discipline he learned in the Army or just how hard-core the man is, but he makes winter in Pin Cherry look like summer in the Caribbean. Hopefully, it will actually warm up around here for the party.

The party! I need to stay focused on the crisis at hand, but there must be a hundred things to do for this grandiose birthday that Mitzy's grandmother, and her team, is planning. I have a special role to play, but if I can't wrap up this robbery and throw these idiots in jail, there's definitely going to be a last-minute change of plans.

Paulsen sets the food delivery down as instructed, but she doesn't retreat. Instead, she jogs out of sight of the bank windows, drops to the icy sidewalk and low-crawls back toward the delivery. I press my mic and hiss. "That's not what we discussed, Paulsen."

She doesn't respond, and I can't push my luck.

If she makes a sound, one of the gunmen could overhear. My plans for a peaceful exchange will go straight out the window.

Paulsen turns her head toward me and gives me a non-verbal go sign. Shaking my head, I pick up the bullhorn. "The food has been delivered. Send out the hostage."

The door opens. The face that pops into the opening is a welcome sight.

My eyes drink in the sight of Mitzy in her curve-hugging skinny jeans and one of her classic T-shirts. There's a picture of a kitten tangled in yarn. Beside the image, the text reads, "Wildly Un-prepared For The Day Ahead."

I want to smile and wave like a silly schoolboy, but I stuff my emotions down and keep it profes-sional. Raising the bullhorn to my lips, I attempt a nonchalant tone. "Keep your hands where we can see them, Miss Moon."

She immediately stops and puts a fist on her hip. "Rude!"

That one gesture tells me all I need to know. She has everything under control inside the bank. My heartbeat returns to almost normal and, for the first time today, I dare to hope for a positive outcome.

She crouches near the full milk crate, and I

watch as she leans toward Deputy Paulsen. Based on body language, there seems to be a hushed exchange.

A pair of white ears peeps into the open doorway, and I hear the voice of one of the gunmen. "Hurry up! Or we shoot one of the hostages."

Boomer's calm voice comes over the radio. "Green light, Sheriff? I've got the shot."

"Negative. Do not take the shot." I can't risk getting Mitzy caught in the crossfire.

Mitzy picks up the crate, turns toward me, and flashes *five* with her left hand. She adjusts the crate and flashes *four* with her right.

We know the armed gang consists of five members, so the four must indicate the remaining hostages.

She takes one step, pretends to stumble, or possibly she actually stumbles—she is adorably clumsy —and flashes *two* with her left hand.

Five gunmen, four hostages, and two? Two what?

She adjusts the crate, makes a weird wiggly motion with her left hand and ducks back inside.

Are there two more hostages? That doesn't make sense. If they were hostages, she would've included it in the count on the right hand.

What am I saying? I have no idea what she was trying to communicate with all the finger gestures.

The hostage exchange proceeds. A woman stumbles forward. It's Cheryl, Deputy Paulsen's mother. She honestly doesn't look as terrified as I would've assumed. When she steps into the harsh sunlight, she immediately wraps her arms around herself and shivers.

Paulsen lies stock still, and the door remains open.

"Boomer, report." I hold my breath.

"No shot. I repeat, no shot."

Well, at least I know my eyes aren't deceiving me. Once Cheryl reaches our side of the street, I motion her to come toward me and send her into the sheriff's station to be debriefed. All the while keeping my eyes locked on that door, as Mitzy swings it closed.

Tabling the cryptic message, I move on to what we need to do to get another hostage released. A couple of minutes pass, and I place a call to her phone.

"Hey, Sheriff. Thanks for the fries."

"You're welcome, Moon. Did you miscount the hostages? Or were those extra fries for you? By the way, you're on an open line being recorded by dispatch."

"Thanks for the warning." Her easy laughter fills my heart with relief.

"Do they have that list of demands together?"

"It's short and simple. They want a bus with a full tank of gas and curtains on all the windows. When it's ready, they want it pulled down the alley, and they'll leave the remaining two hostages in the bank when they board the bus."

There goes my blood pressure. "But there are three hostages remaining, Miss Moon."

"You're not wrong, C— C— sweetie. But I'm their ticket out of town. Once they're across the border, they'll set me—"

The call ends abruptly, and my head is spinning. Across the border? They can't possibly be headed for Mexico. I might not open fire on them for the sake of my girlfriend, but if they're headed for Mexico, there are a multitude of states between here and there where the authorities won't take so kindly to fugitive armed robbers.

Wait . . . C-C-sweetie? She wasn't stuttering. CC! My buddy in the Canadian Mounties! They want to head for Canada. That tells me two things. They're listening to Mitzy more than anyone should, and they don't have a solid grasp of international law. Canada and the US have an extradition treaty. But what they don't know won't hurt my gal.

"Dispatch, get on the horn with the bus service to secure a vehicle, and tap Clarence to find out how long it'll take him to kit out the set of wheels."

Now my only job is to keep the heat low on this pressure cooker of a situation and make sure the remaining hostages are left alive in the bank when the gunmen board their getaway vehicle—with Mitzy.

CHAPTER 8

DEEP DOWN, I've always believed that french fries can fix anything. Munching on these pieces of golden potato perfection in the middle of an armed bank robbery proves my hypothesis. Everyone, including the criminals, is blissed out on Odell's delicious food. I hadn't even considered the possibility of a food coma solving all of our problems, but as I take in the satisfied expressions throughout the room and imagine the ones beneath the masks, I'm considering believing in miracles.

I hope Erick figures out my crappy sign language. I'm not sure how it will help him to know that there are a couple of ghosts running loose inside the bank, but I always hear people say things like forearmed is forewarned—or maybe it's the opposite. As my full belly releases some happiness endorphins, I can almost hear Gene Wilder's Willy Wonka say, "Scratch that, reverse it."

The White Rabbit interrupts my mental gymnastics. "How long do you think it'll take your boyfriend to get our ride?"

For a moment I hesitate, then I remember that talking with my mouth full is hardly going to be the worst crime committed today. "There's not a bus station in town. Which means the closest one is probably in Broken Rock. That's about a half hour away. Then we need to factor in the time to fill the tank, put up some kind of coverings over the windows, and get it parked in the alley . . . I think we're looking at anywhere from an hour to an hour and a half. Why?"

"You think they're on the level?"

Slurping down some soda, I wipe my mouth with the back of my hand. "What do you mean?"

"Will they get the bus? Are they just dragging their feet until we let our guard down, or do you think they'll let us drive away?"

Wow, either these guys have never seen a single heist movie, or they've had an unusually good run of luck and assumed they'd never get caught. "Sheriff Harper is a straight shooter."

Five comical masks turn toward me in unison.

Waving my hands to fend off their overreaction, I have another go at my response. "That came out wrong. I meant it like, he's honest. If he says he's getting you a bus, he's getting you a bus."

As the rabbit maneuvers another handful of fries beneath his mask, I catch a glimpse of his blond mustache. I'll lock that tidbit away for later.

"What about you guys? Are you really gonna let me go when you get into Canada?"

For the first time, the Cheshire Cat speaks to me directly. "I dunno, Mitzy. You seem to have a knack for this sort of thing. Are you sure you don't wanna stick with the gang?"

I wish this had been the first time I'd been offered a chance to join an armed crew, and I hope this operation turns out better than that one. Loss of life, no matter whose, never sits well with me. "I appreciate the offer, Smiley. Honestly, I do. But I've got a lot going on here, you know."

Alice lifts her mask to take a bite of her burger and, unfortunately, reveals most of her face. I'm not exactly saying I could pick her out of a lineup, but her youthful face and the distinct mole on her left cheek are definitely emblazoned in my mind. "Like, what do you do around here?" she asks as she munches on her cheeseburger.

Rather than make myself sound too well off, I try to keep my story blue-collar. "I work at a bookshop."

Unfortunately, the middle-aged bank employee

who I offended earlier is either seeking revenge, or he's simply dense. "Don't sell yourself short, Miss Moon. She owns the bookstore and runs a generous philanthropic organization."

Blerg.

The White Rabbit sets down his soda and picks up his gun. "Things just got interesting. Not only do we have the perfect ticket out of town, but once we're safely on the other side of the border, we can ransom you for some additional dough."

Murmurs of agreement grumble through the gang.

If looks could kill, the glare I'm shooting Mr. Blabbermouth should drop him dead on the spot. His wide eyes and pale complexion, coupled with my special abilities, confirm his *blurt* was accidental.

"You're in charge, Mr. Rabbit. Although, the more you complicate things, the more opportunity you give law enforcement to catch up with you. Sheriff Harper is playing it cool, because he's interested in making sure all the hostages, including me, make it out safely. However, he's not a pushover. If you test him, you'll regret it."

The energy in the room shifts instantaneously, and I realize my mistake too late. Befriending the group was one thing, but publicly opposing their leader—not a good plan.

Me and my big mouth.

"Hatter, you got another one of those zip ties. Seems like doll face is getting a little too big for her britches."

As usual, my tendency to laugh in the face of danger takes over, and a chuckle escapes my lips before I have a chance to stifle it.

"You think that's funny, blondie?" Once again, he tucks the gun under my chin and presses it threateningly.

I offer my response through clenched teeth. "It wasn't funny. I have a real problem with authority. Plus, *big for my britches*, you know." I risk a pat toward my backside and, thankfully, Alice gets the joke.

"Ease up, Ears. She didn't mean anything by it. She, like, helped us out, you know. Just pump the brakes."

For once, I know when to keep my mouth shut.

Mr. Rabbit backs away and withdraws the gun from my chin, but doesn't return to his meal.

The initial survival instinct and the burning desire to fight back are hard to resist. But I think there's more to gain by cooperating. The Mad Hatter hands him a zip tie, and Mr. Rabbit secures it around my wrists. He leads me into the bank manager's office, shoves me roughly into a chair, and closes the door behind him when he leaves.

It's a good news-bad news situation. Good news: I have my phone in my back pocket and the blinds on the manager's office window are already lowered. Bad news: I have my phone in my back pocket, and my hands are secured behind my back.

Now, my attorney/alchemist Silas Willoughby taught me a transmutation for getting myself out of metal handcuffs ages ago, but I'm not sure if the same properties would apply to plastic zip ties.

RING.

No time to wonder.

RING.

I have to get that phone out of my pocket and answer that call before it rings again. Erick isn't going to take kindly to being ignored in this tense situation.

Fortunately, I'm good with my hands. Don't worry, a "that's what she said" floated through my brain too.

Sliding the phone from my pocket, I tap what I'm hoping is the right part of the screen, twist my head over my shoulder, and offer my greeting. "Hey, Sheriff. Sorry for the delay. I'm a little tied up."

The voice that sounds from my phone is not the one I expected. "Mizithra? Is this one of your attempts at comedy or are you sincerely in peril?"

"Silas! I'm so glad it's you. I'm being held

hostage by the White Rabbit, and there are two ghosts loose in the bank. Honestly, I don't know what to do."

"Oh, heavens. I fear you may have inhaled the smoke from one of those funny cigarettes I've heard about."

Classic Silas. I should've known better than to spout off a series of pop culture references without the proper etiquette. "It's not a drug-induced hallucination. There's literally an armed robbery at Pin Cherry Harbor Bank & Trust. There are five armed robbers all dressed like characters from Alice in Wonderland, three hostages including myself, and two ghosts!"

He harrumphs, and I can easily picture him smoothing his bushy grey mustache with a thumb and forefinger. However, the image of his jowls jiggling as he chuckles at my predicament is totally unexpected.

"Silas, this is no laughing matter. Right now my hands are zip-tied behind my back in the manager's office. They're threatening to kill a hostage if Erick doesn't meet their demands."

"It continues to be a surprising pleasure to speak with you, Mitzy. You may use the transmutation I taught you to remove the binding from your wrists. It may require more intense focus, but your abilities have expanded and I have faith in your success."

"All right. That's one problem solved. What about the ghosts? One of them is one of the original bank robbers. He might've killed more than one person back then."

A low grumbling spills from the phone and my clairsentience tingles with my mentor's concern. "This would be the infamous robbery gone wrong. The one that resulted in the death of Fred Clements."

"Is that the robber or the security guard?"

"Fred was the security guard and an old backgammon companion. The two of us wiled away dozens of Sunday afternoons over snifters of brandy and the backgammon board." A melancholy sigh escapes. "In fact, he knew Jedediah. They shared a love for the sport of golf."

There's no time for me to point out that an activity that involves standing on grass and riding in a cart doesn't sound like a sport. However, the mention of Silas's older brother does spark a psychic flutter. "Silas, you said 'knew Jedediah.' Was the past tense in reference to Fred, or did your brother cross over?"

"Indeed. My brother's transition was peaceful and our last days together were filled with fond reminiscing. There was an intimate service with his closest friends. He left most of his estate to his favorite animal rescue and a scholarly research grant at his alma mater. My call was meant to inform you of my return to Pin Cherry tomorrow. Although, I will make a future trip to his home to collect the treasured tomes he left me."

"I honestly want to hear the entire story, Silas, but I don't know how much time I have until they come back in. I think I can handle the gang, but what do I do about the ghosts?"

"Mizithra, I hate to sound like an impaired Victrola vinyl, but you must do what you always do. Discover their unfinished business and help them cross over."

"But—"

*CHAPTER 9*

THE HANDLE ON THE DOOR to the bank manager's office slowly twists. I end the call and struggle to shove the phone back into my pocket.

When the door opens, I'm surprised to see the cheery mask of Alice rather than the rabbit's ears. "Mitzy? That's your name, right?"

"Yeah, that's my name. Come on in, Alice."

"No. Can't. I don't want Ears to see me. But, um, I just need to say that the guys are, like, getting antsy. And there's more super extra stuff happening. You know, with the lights and the temperature dropping. You were totally keeping them calm."

Now's my chance. "Alice, I know how weird this is going to sound, but do you believe in ghosts?"

For a moment, it appears her plastic mask has gained the ability to change its expression. She nods fervently. "Totally. Ever since my Nan passed, there's been— Things have happened. But is that what you think this is? For reals?"

"I'm no expert." Far be it from me to share my actual paranormal experience with my captors. "But what other explanation is there? I mean, I said the stuff about the building shifting, or whatever, because I didn't want the Mad Hatter shooting anyone. Honestly, though, I think it's ghosts."

Alice places a hand over the mouth on her mask. "Unfinished business. My Nan talked about that all the time before she died. She was, like, obsessed with finishing all her business. She didn't want to be trapped, you know?"

"I think you're right. You need to get me back out there. Maybe the two of us can figure out what their unfinished business is and get them out of here."

Alice nods her blonde plastic locks. "I'll talk to Ears. Sometimes he actually listens to me."

"Good luck."

She steps out of the room, and I'm tempted to try my hand at the transmutation Silas mentioned. However, I have no idea what will actually happen to the plastic band, and if it melts or something, I'd have a hard time explaining that. I'll hold off and see if Alice can work some magic on that darn bunny.

Hopefully Erick sent someone to update Twiggy, and maybe Grams will overhear. Yeesh, what am I worried about! News travels faster than light in this town. If Ghost-ma wasn't tethered to that bookshop, she'd already be here—cracking skulls.

This time, the door opens with forceful confidence. "Alice said she needs your help. You believe this nonsense?"

Not having the benefit of knowing which nonsense he's referring to, I keep my mouth shut and nod my head.

He stomps over, grabs a pair of scissors from the pen cup on the desk, and cuts the zip tie from my wrists.

"Thank you." Wow! I can't believe I didn't see the scissors. Here I was gearing up for some grand alchemical working, when there was a pair of scissors literally within reach.

"No funny business. No calls unless I say so."

It takes every ounce of self-control I don't possess to keep from giggling at a giant rabbit telling me "no funny business." Yet, somehow, I manage. "Copy that."

He storms out of the office and I follow in what I hope is a timid fashion. Alice is waiting outside. She grabs my hand and pulls me toward the hallway. "It started downstairs. I think we should creep back to the vault."

I glance over my shoulder and clock the security guard still sitting with the two remaining hostages and nod my head toward the basement. However, the masked disco delinquent is nowhere to be seen. "Sounds good. Do I lead or follow?"

She shrugs. "There's room to walk side by side."

Falling in step beside her, she presses her shoulder close as we head down to the old vault.

My mood ring is lifeless. There's no tingling on the back of my neck. I don't think the ghost guy is down here.

Stepping into the vault, Alice aims the light on her phone all around the corners. Nothing happens, so she assumes no ghosts.

However, when the beam scans the far corner, I see the ghost of the gunman, unmasked, wiping tears from his eyes.

"Total waste. There's nothing here, Mitzy. Let's head back upstairs."

"You go ahead. I'll hang out for another minute and see if anything happens."

She shivers visibly and steps back. "Cool. Sounds good. I'll hang at the back door with Queenie."

"All right. I'll come and find you in a few."

She backs out of the tomb-like vault and footsteps race to the upper floor. Complete darkness envelops me, and my heart races as I take a seat on the floor. "Hey, I know you're in here. I can help you. I don't have a lot of time to explain and I can't let anyone else know that I can see you, but I can help."

A soft glow emanates from the corner, and the formerly masked gunman floats expectantly toward me. "Hey, pretty lady. You sure you're not trippin'?"

"I'm not trippin'. I can see you."

"Groovy."

His vocabulary seems out of sync with his wardrobe. Although, if he grew up in the '60s, it kind of makes sense. Still, the wardrobe screams *Saturday Night Fever*. I can almost picture the gold cross dangling from a chain around his neck.

"Hey, seems like you have some regrets about what happened. Is that your unfinished business?"

"Regrets? Sure, I guess. I been chillin' in this bank with the guy I killed for over fifty years. It kinda had an effect on me. I just wanna keep on truckin', but —"

"Fate had other plans?"

"Right on, sister."

"Well, have you told Mr. Clements how you feel?"

"You know it. I apologized and everything. So,

why am I still here? It's a bummer, man. I don't get it."

"I've heard bits and pieces of the story. Sounds like more than one person was killed. Is it possible that you're responsible for more than one murder?"

His glowing eyes turn black. The frightening image of a hovering ghost with two soulless black holes for eyes causes my chest to tighten and my stomach to pitch.

"I never shot that lady. You hear? It wasn't me."

I raise both of my hands in surrender. "Hey, I'm not saying it was. I'm here to help. Remember?"

"Yeah, I don't blame the youngbloods. I would've done the same. We all said as much at breakfast that morning, you know?"

"Said what?" My head tilts with interest.

"If somebody goes down, we dump all the heavy stuff on them. Nobody dies in vain. No questions."

"All right. So you died, and they said you were the mastermind behind the whole robbery and that you shot all the people. Wouldn't ballistics have proven that the bullet didn't come from your gun?"

The blackness in his eyes is replaced by flickering flames. "You the fuzz? You pigs trying to trick me into a confession?"

"Hey, you're dead. Confession or not, you already paid the ultimate price." Taking a deep breath, I try a different approach. "What's your name?"

"Donnie. What's yours, foxy mama?"

"It's Mitzy." I choose to ignore the inappropriate comment. "Look, Donnie, I want to help you. I'm not a cop. Full disclosure, though, I am dating the current sheriff. But he doesn't know anything about this. All right?"

Donnie adjusts his snug polyester bellbottoms and tugs at the large points of his shirt's collar. "We're cool."

"So, tell me how you got blamed for murdering the woman."

"The lady was crying about her kid at home and made a run for the door. Tiny Tim threatened her and the security guard pulled out a back-up piece."

"This woman, was it Lindy McElroy?"

"S'pose it was. I heard plenty a talk—after I died." Donnie shrugs and continues. "I thought the rent-a-cop was gonna light up my buddy." He wipes a hand across his mouth. "I shot him and he got one off before he hit the dirt."

"Did the guard mean to shoot you, or was he still aiming at Tiny Tim?"

"Who knows? Tiny Tim shot that lady, but I shot the guard."

Hugging my knees to my chest, I lean toward the disco ghost. "Then what happened?"

"Tiny Tim tried to save me. We were tight. But the guard musta nicked an artery when he lit me up. I was bleedin' out fast. One minute I was sound as a pound and next I'm slipping away. Tiny Tim wanted to get me to my feet, but the whole room was spinning. I told him to peace out, and I asked him to take care of Shelly for me."

My insufferable snoopiness interjects. "Was Shelly your old lady?"

"Yeah. She was the best." He wipes an ethereal tear from the corner of his eye and continues. "Things got foggy real fast, but I think Tiny Tim put his gun in my other hand."

"So you died in the bank with a gun in each hand. As far as the cops knew, you killed everybody."

"Yeah. They threw it all on me. Just like we planned." His harsh empty laughter says he's no longer a fan of the plan that seemed flawless when he was alive.

"Donnie, I promise if you help me protect these hostages. I'll clear your name once this robbery is over."

"Whaddya take me for? You might be a stone fox, but I know you're only trying to save your own neck."

"Look, I don't like to brag, buddy, but I've solved a bunch of murders and other cases since I came to this town. And I happen to specialize in helping earthbound spirits cross over."

"Oh yeah? Like who?"

"I can't break my confidentiality. Part of my service is keeping the secrets I'm asked to keep." Not that any of that is true, but thankfully Donnie the disco burglar can't read my thoughts like Grams.

He nods, and his expression is dead serious. "I respect that. I'll help you—on one condition."

We all saw this coming, right? "What's your condition?"

"If I smell a rat, your little friend Tilly is—" He draws a finger across his neck in the internationally understood sign for murder.

"Understood. I double-cross you, Tilly pays the price. No problem. I always keep my word."

"What now, broad?" Donnie drifts absently around the dank, musty vault.

"I need to make sure you've changed your ways. You hustle up to the lobby and send Fred down, so I can brief him. I can't be seen talking to ghosts up there." I point toward the main floor.

Let it not be said that Donnie lost his sense of humor over the years. He takes my command seriously and launches into a spotless rendition of the Hustle. Mind you, my only reference is John Travolta's version, but Donnie does him proud as he dances his way out of the bank tomb.

The silence presses against my eardrums, and Erick's face fills my mind. Note to self: I may have uncovered the number one reason I'm avoiding having an honest discussion with Erick. If I promise to tell him the truth, I'll have to *keep* my promise.

## CHAPTER 10 — ERICK

I SHOULD'VE HEARD from Mitzy by now. Something's gone wrong. I know it. "Paulsen."

The small but tough deputy strides over and avoids eye contact. "Yes, Sheriff."

"We'll discuss your breach of protocol during the food delivery later. I'm gonna head inside and debrief Cheryl. I need you to take point on this operation."

"10-4." She swallows hard and looks up. "I know it wasn't protocol, Sheriff. I just wanted to find out if my mom was—"

I can't say I've ever seen weakness of any kind from Deputy Paulsen. But the emotion that tightens her throat and steals her words is palpable. Leaning forward, I lower my voice. "Hey, Pauly. Don't worry about it. You run things out here, and I'll make sure she's taken care of. We got her out safe. That's all that matters."

Deputy Paulsen's eyes speak volumes, but now isn't the time to push. Her right hand grips the handle of her gun and she nods sternly.

We both ignore the tears welling in her eyes.

"Sheriff, do I have the authority to give Boomer the green light?"

"Negative. If they shoot first, all bets are off. Otherwise, nobody takes a shot till I get back."

"10-4."

Leaving my capable deputy in charge, I head indoors for a hot cup of coffee and hopefully some insight.

Paulsen's mother sits in the bullpen with a wool blanket tucked around her shoulders and a steaming cup of joe in her hands.

"Cheryl, I sure was glad to see you walk out of that bank."

"You and me both, Ricky."

The nickname brings a self-conscious flush to my face. I forget how much time she and my mother spend together. Somehow, when my mom calls me Ricky, I can let it slide like water off a duck's back, but I can't have my deputies picking up on that handle. "It's Sheriff Harper when we're in the station, ma'am."

Her mouth opens in genuine shock and she nods. "Oh, you betcha. You betcha, Sheriff."

"You look pretty comfortable where you're at, Cheryl. Is it okay if I debrief you, here, in the bullpen?"

"Of course, Ri— Sheriff. I've got no secrets from you and my Pauly."

Taking out my trusty pen and pad, I pull up a chair. "We already have some of this information. But I want to go through the basics and make sure we didn't miss anything. How many armed robbers?"

"Well, now. I suppose there's five. But I'm not sure if that sweet little Alice is packing any heat. I can't say as I saw a gun. But there's definitely five in the crew."

"Okay. How many hostages?"

"Gosh! There was Tilly, and me, and Mr. Curb, and that blabbermouth Jeff, and, of course, your sweet Mitzy. My goodness, she's awful calm under pressure. I can see why the two of you are such a good match."

It's going to be harder to keep her on topic than I thought. "So, five hostages in total. Tilly's been released. Of course, you're here. That leaves Mitzy, Jeff, and Mr. Curb inside. Is that correct?"

"Oh, Sheriff, you don't have to take that formal tone with me. I'm not a suspect, am I?"

"Of course not, Cheryl. I just wanted to make sure I heard you correctly. Seems like Mitzy indicated there could be some additional hostages. She was trying to signal me when she picked up the food, but I've clearly misunderstood."

Cheryl tugs the blanket tight around her shoulders and leans forward. Her eyes widen and her voice is barely audible. "Well now, she might have been referring to the poltergeist."

You could knock me over with a feather. "A poltergeist?"

Mrs. Paulsen nods in complete seriousness. "Every once in a while, strange things happen at the bank. Mr. Curb always tries to brush it off, but I can see the truth in his eyes. He knows they aren't just accidents. Like today! A whole stack of those deposit slips flew up in the air. Now, he'd have to think I fell off the turnip truck yesterday to believe a wind came through the bank all willy-nilly."

Mrs. Paulsen's wild tale sheds a whole new light on Mitzy's signal. Two. The two and the wiggling hand: two ghosts. I'm not sure I would've figured it out without Cheryl's tipoff, but the wiggly hand gesture from *Wayne's World* might've sunk through my thick skull at some point. "So there's a poltergeist in the bank. Interesting."

"Now, don't look at me like that, Ricky. Sorry,

Sheriff. I'm not pulling your leg. You remember when that gunshot went off, don't you?"

I attempt to keep the worry from my face as I nod.

"Dontcha know, one of the typewriters flew right off a desk. There wasn't a soul around it. Well, no *living* soul! I'm telling you, the poltergeist knocked that typewriter off. And if the silly Mad Hatter hadn't been such a bad shot . . . Gosh, someone could've been seriously injured."

"So the Mad Hatter is the one watching the front door?"

"That's right. And I'll tell you something else. I think he's out of ammunition. I've got real good hearing. Ask Pauly. After he fired that second shot, I saw him slink over to the White Rabbit and they thought they were whispering, but ol' Cheryl picked up a thing or two." She taps her left ear with a finger and continues. "He was out of ammunition. I know they looked around for some spare, but I don't think they found any."

"Well, thank you for telling me that." Her tip isn't enough to have me risk storming the place, but it's something to think about. "You said there were five. Alice, the White Rabbit, the Mad Hatter, and who else?"

"Let's see . . . One young man is dressed up as the Queen of Hearts. And then there's a boy in a

Cheshire Cat mask. He's the one they said got arrested for boosting a car. Is that the right term, Sheriff? Boosting?"

"It's one of them, Cheryl. Can you tell me anything about their voices, or did you see any of their hands?"

"No hands. Whoever put those getups together thought of everything. They all have gloves. And their voices sound regular. You know, like they're from around here. Not nearby, 'course. More like city folk. But not far. You know what else I thought of, Sheriff?"

Cheryl Paulsen is an unstoppable force, so I best let my informant roll on. "What's that?"

"I don't think it's any accident that they've robbed the Pin Cherry Harbor Bank & Trust. Round here about everyone knows we don't have a security guard." She waves that tidbit away and chuckles. "But guess what else? It's not a chain. Well, not a national chain. Because, you know, if they were knocking off those big-name branches, the Feds would have been here in a heartbeat."

"That's an excellent point, Cheryl. I sure do appreciate all your helpful observations. Let me update the team, and see if I can find someone to drive you home."

"Oh pshaw! I'm not going to waste your manpower on giving me a ride home, Sheriff. I'm happy as a lark right here. In fact, why don't I pop into the diner and get you some food? I'm sure the lot of you must be half starved. You can't survive on donuts alone."

When my cell phone rings, I answer immediately. "Sheriff Harper."

"Hey, Erick. Did you miss me?"

No matter what my heart screams, I have to maintain a professional attitude. "Let's remember you're on a recorded line, Miss Moon."

"Copy that. I've only got a couple of seconds before they check on me. I'm downstairs by the old vault."

"Okay. Are the hostages all okay?"

"They were when I left. Did you get my hand signals?"

Whew! Somehow I have to let her know I figured out the part about the ghosts, without announcing to everyone listening that the local sheriff believes in poltergeists. "I did. After I talked to Cheryl and heard more about the typewriter and the deposit slips, I figured it all out." Mitzy is pretty sharp, she'll know what I mean.

"Cracked the code, eh, Sheriff?"

Despite the tension, she pulls a small chuckle from me. "Anything to report?"

"Someone's coming. I gotta go. Just wanted to hear your voice."

The call ends and my heart sinks.

My coffee is cold, the donuts are stale, and I have a bad feeling about this bus option.

Maybe I should call her back and see if we can come up with some kind of excuse to release another hostage. I hit the number and the call rings several times.

"Oh hello, Sheriff. Been a while since we talked."

"Yes. I'm calling to give you an update on the bus. It's proving difficult to find window coverings. It could delay delivery of the vehicle for another hour."

"Hold on, Sheriff." Mitzy must've turned away or put her hand over the phone.

Muffled voices, raised voices, Mitzy's calm tone, and she's back. "The White Rabbit said if you can get the bus here in thirty minutes he'll release another hostage."

"Any chance that hostage will be you?"

"Not unless Hades has suddenly frozen over, Sheriff. Can you do it?"

"I can get it here in thirty minutes with no curtains. Do we have a deal?"

A bit more mumbling filters through the phone before Mitzy returns. "That's affirmative, Sheriff. No curtains. Thirty minutes. You get a hostage."

The line goes dead.

Throwing my jacket on as I head outside, I offer an update to Deputy Paulsen. "So, I'm going to head over to Clarence's shop and give him the new specs. There was no answer when I called. Plus, maybe there's something I can do to speed things along. I definitely want to make it in under that thirty-minute window and get another hostage out of there."

"10-4. Sorry it won't be Moon, Sheriff."

"That makes two of us. I'll let you know when the bus is on the move."

Paulsen nods and picks up the bullhorn with her left hand.

As I walk to the end of the street to grab one of the extra vehicles from the Broken Rock station, Paulsen's voice echoes loud and strong down the laneway as she updates the armed crew about their new point of contact.


**"WHAT'S UP, CLARENCE?** How goes the remodel?"

"Not as easy as you might think, Sheriff. I've only got enough of this sheeting to cover half the windows on one side. It's gonna be hours before I get my hands on some more."

Resting a hand on his grease-streaked shoulder, I give it a squeeze. "Then I've got some good news, buddy. No curtains required. I cut a deal with the crooks to release another hostage if I get the bus there in under thirty minutes."

"Fine by me, Sheriff. I already rigged the gas tank. She looks full as can be, but there's barely two gallons in there! You can hop in and drive it over right now."

"Good to know. There are a couple of things I wanted you to do before you take it over. Shouldn't take you more than twenty to twenty-five minutes, if you're as good as they say." I gesture toward his massive collection of tools as I throw down the challenge.

Clarence tugs his beanie down over his ears and crosses his arms over his puffed-up chest. "Oh, you know I'm that good. What can I do ya for, Sheriff?"

## CHAPTER 11

Unfortunately, Alice and the White Rabbit come downstairs before Disco Donnie convinces the security guard to pay me a visit. With the time frame getting mashed down to thirty minutes, that doesn't give me much of a chance to figure out what the security guard's unfinished business might be.

The White Rabbit waves the tip of his handgun in the light cast from a cell phone. "Let's head back upstairs. And no more field trips without my permission. Understood, Alice?"

"Yeah. You bet, Ears. You're in charge."

We all head back to the main lobby.

To be fair, Donnie is talking the security guard's ear off, and as soon as I get to the top of the stairs Fred peeks around his frenemy's apparition to double-check the story.

Nodding as casually as I can, I hope to encourage the guard to trust me. Queenie was still at the back door when we passed. The Mad Hatter has a lock on the front door and windows, and the Cheshire Cat sits cross-legged on a desk, staring at the two seated hostages.

Hoping that the landline is being monitored by dispatch—or someone—I walk toward that desk and lean against it with my back screening the telephone and the dangling receiver.

The White Rabbit hasn't noticed the breach yet, so I attempt to get some potentially helpful information for the law enforcement officers camped outside. "Hey, did you find any ammunition for Hatter?"

The fuzzy white ears tilt sideways. "Why do you ask? You wearin' a wire?"

"Me? Wearing a wire? Like as an everyday accessory? I came into the bank to get some money for the register at my bookshop. I didn't know I was going to be a pawn in a robbery gone wrong." Bad choice of words.

"Hey, it hasn't gone wrong. We got our getaway vehicle on the way and we got our ticket out of town right here." He raises the gun toward my head.

"Then I'd advise you to be careful with that thing. If you mess up this ticket"—I wave a hand at my person—"more than the robbery is going to go wrong." Last time I popped off, I ended up in a zip tie. This time, he lowers the gun and nods. Apparently, I've made more headway than I thought.

"If they don't make it in under thirty, I'm taking out the one called Jeff." Rabbit waves his gun toward the other two hostages.

"Understood. Like I told you before, Sheriff Harper doesn't make promises he can't keep. The bus will be here. Don't worry."

Alice and Ears both nod.

Time to make one last attempt at gathering intel. "I'm trying to come up with the best order of loading onto the bus. When you guys come out of the bank, you're going to be targets. I was asking about Hatter's ammunition so we know who can take a strategic position, and who can't."

The fuzzy ears bob up and down thoughtfully. "I like the way you think, Mitzy. The Hatter's totally out. The spare shotgun shells were in the van. His gun is a prop at this point."

Dear Lord baby Jesus! I hope someone important heard that. "Got it. Then you better put him on me."

Alice's painted-on grin nods excitedly. "That's brilliant. The cops won't know Hatter's out of ammunition, and if anything goes down, the rest of us can return fire."

"You're packing, Alice?"

She pats the pocket of her apron, and I have to figure out a way to convey this information out loud. "You had a gun in the pocket of your apron this whole time? Wow! I never saw you pull it out. Nicely done."

She takes a mock bow and the White Rabbit checks the time on his phone. "They've got ten minutes, Mitzy. You better call."

"Sure. No problem." Pulling my phone out of my pocket, I tap speed dial for Sheriff Harper. There are several strange clicks and a disappointing ending.

"Deputy Paulsen for Sheriff Harper."

"Where's Erick?" That question wasn't for the gang of armed robbers, it was strictly for me.

"He went over to the garage to give Clarence the news to eighty-six the curtains. There was no answer when he called and he didn't want to lose any time. He put me in charge. What's going on?"

"They want an update. Time is running out. Is the bus on its way?"

Paulsen must put the call on mute, because the line goes silent. The gang fidgets, but in a moment she hops back on. "The bus is en route. When it arrives, send the exchange hostage out the front door, before you board."

"No problem. We'll send Jeff out. We're leaving Mr. Curb in the bank, and the Mad Hatter will have his shotgun firmly planted in my back when the rest of us get on the bus."

She scoffs.

"Hey, Paulsen, I know you're not too concerned about whether I make it out of this in one piece or not, but I'm under the impression that Erick is. So, tell your sniper to pull back. Nobody takes a shot at the crew. My life is on the line. You heard that, right? The Mad Hatter's double-barrel shotgun in the middle of my back. Can I be any clearer? Or do you need to call dispatch and have them play it back for you?" Ending the call with a huff, I shove my phone into my pocket with unnecessary force.

I hope they bought that performance.

The White Rabbit lowers his gun and nods. "I heard Smiley offer you a position on the crew. I'll double down on that. You got a real skill for negotiating. Compared to most women, you've got nerves of steel."

Pressing my lips together to stifle a smug grin, I nod in what I hope passes for humble acceptance.

He bought it.

Of course, the weak link in the chain is hoping that Deputy Paulsen can unravel my cryptic message and will review the dispatch tapes. If they're monitoring the call from Tilly's desk on a recorded line, they'll know that the gun in the middle of my back is empty.

Translation: they can take all the sniper shots they want.

With the few minutes I have remaining, I need to talk to Fred Clements. An otherworldly distraction would be mighty helpful. I hope Disco Donnie is smarter than he looks. "Hey, Ears, I know the whole ghost thing sounds weird, but I'd hate for them to throw some kind of monkey wrench into your final getaway."

Luckily, Donnie picks up what I'm laying down, and knocks over one of the gold stanchions holding a short length of velvet rope beside the empty customer queue.

The White Rabbit jumps and shakes his long ears. "Make it snappy, and Alice is gonna escort you down there."

"Copy that." Grabbing my puffy coat from the nearby desk, I gesture for Alice to follow me.

At the top of the steps, she hesitates and clenches my arm. "Mitzy?"

"Yeah, what's wrong?"

"This ghost is, like, really scaring me. Can you go down to the vault by yourself? I'll stay right here at the top of the stairs. Ears doesn't have to know."

I couldn't have planned this better—if I'd planned it. I'll promise to keep her little secret, and now I might get a favor in return. "Totally. I'm not thrilled about it myself. Um, I noticed you're not super into guns."

"Yeah, not even!" Alice rolled her eyes.

Now for my last-ditch play.

A couple weeks ago, Silas had instructed me to study an old tome containing barely readable essays on persuasive speech. I've slogged through about half of it, but I can't practice on Grams or Pyewacket. Technically, I could practice on Twiggy —but if she ever found out, she'd send me to join Ghost-ma in the "in between" without a second thought! No time like the present . . . "Alice, would you mind giving me your gun in case things go sideways down there?" I think I have the tone and pacing correct. Fingers crossed.

Once again, I can almost swear her plastic mask is capable of expressions. A wave of relief rolls off her. "OMG. I hate carrying a gun. I've never used one yet. In fact, you should just keep it. If something goes down when we're loading into that bus, I'm not going to be the one to, like, shoot back. You know what I'm saying?"

"Absolutely. No one has to know. We're cool."

She nods and hands me her gun.

"Thanks." I aim the gun at nothing as I creep down the stairwell toward the darkened vault. As soon as I'm past her sight line, I check the safety and tuck the gun into the back of my waistband—

hidden under my puffy coat. The naïve ingénue, Alice, might trust me, but I'm pretty sure the White Rabbit would frown on one of his hostages having a firearm.

As soon as I walk past the thick metal door, I feel a presence. "Mr. Clements, is that you?"

He barely shimmers in the darkness. "Donnie says you can fix things. Why should I believe him, or you?"

"Mr. Clements, I'm a very good friend of Silas Willoughby. He said the two of you passed many an evening over snifters of brandy and a backgammon table. I'm not sure how much you know about his extracurricular activities, but he believes in my ability to help earthbound spirits cross over."

It's as though someone slowly slides up a dimmer switch, and Fred's ethereal form glows with increased intensity. "You know Silas? Is that ol' dog still alive?"

"He is. He's probably going to outlive all of us." Oops, open mouth, insert foot. Obviously, he's already outlived Fred.

Lucky for me, Fred assumes the joke was intentional. As he laughs, his image solidifies before me.

"Look, Fred, we don't have a lot of time. Tell me what happened that day in the bank?"

He stares at me, and his apparition immediately dims.

"Listen, I'm not here to judge you. Donnie already told me his version, but I need to hear your side of the story. I can help you. I promise."

"It was a Wednesday, not that it matters. Every day was the same. Efficient staff, pleasant locals, and me locking up."

"But something different happened this Wednesday."

He nervously tucks his uniform shirt into his pants. "They came out of nowhere. There were five of them, just like today. There'd never been a robbery at the bank before, and I hadn't fired my gun in almost a decade. You know how it is. Nothing much ever happens in Pin Cherry."

I nod encouragingly and keep my opinions about Pin Cherry to myself.

"Well, that McElroy lady was beside herself. She had a real young babe at home, and she just wouldn't calm down. You know?"

I didn't, but for purposes of expediency, I nod and smile.

"They cleared out the cash drawers in seconds and were gonna force me to take 'em down to the vault. We turned to head toward the stairs, and Lindy made a break for the door. Donnie's friend . . . Of course, I didn't know him at the time, but Donnie and I have done our fair share of chewing the fat in the last fifty years. So now I know the guy's name was Tiny Tim. He aims his gun at Mrs. McElroy, and I reached down to grab my backup piece from my ankle holster." Fred pauses, pats his round belly, and shakes his head. "Now, I'm not as young or as svelte as I used to be, and it took me a second to get that gun and myself situated. But when I had him in my sights, I froze."

"What do you mean?"

"I couldn't do it. Couldn't pull the trigger. My brain was stuck in some kind of loop, you know? Well, Donnie saw me draw down on his buddy, and fired at me. When Donnie's gun went off, ol' Tiny Tim shot that poor lady. Donnie's bullet hit me and I collapsed to my knees. As I went down, I fired. I don't know what I was aiming at."

"But you missed Tiny Tim and shot Donnie instead."

"Sure did. I wasn't trying to get revenge for him shooting me, or anything like that. I wish I woulda shot Tiny Tim. At least I could've avenged poor Mrs. McElroy's death. I was just a damn coward. I've had to live with that every day." He turns away from me and he's barely a flicker.

"What's your biggest regret, Fred?"

"That I didn't take the shot on Tiny Tim. If I'd just taken the shot—"

"There's no way to go back in time. And there's no way to know if the outcome would've been any

different. The bottom line is you helped us out today. You kept this gang on their toes, and, so far, all
the hostages are safe."

"That wasn't me! That's Donnie. He always
thought it was a hoot to mess with humans. Me? I
just creep around in the shadows. Good for nothing
in death, just like I was good for nothing in life."

Maybe if I come at this problem from a different angle, I can get Fred to end his pity party.
"What happened after? Once you were a ghost?"

"Well, I saw that scoundrel Tiny Tim put his
gun in Donnie's left hand. That way, Donnie would
have both guns. The one that shot me and the one
that shot Lindy. They laid the whole thing at his
feet, just like Donnie said they would."

"Look, Fred, I'm going to help Donnie take care
of his unfinished business, and I'm pretty sure that
means convicting the right person of Lindy McElroy's murder. But for you, it seems like something
different is needed. I think you need to be brave. I
think you need to go upstairs and do whatever you
have to do to make sure Jeff and Mr. Curb get out of
this thing unscathed."

"What about you? Once you're on the bus,
there's nothing I can do for you."

"You don't need to take responsibility for me,
Fred. I've always been ten pounds of trouble stuffed
into a five-pound sack. I promise you, if you make

sure Jeff and Mr. Curb get out of this alive, I'll be back to help you cross over."

"Mitzy, come on! The bus is here!" Alice's nervous voice trickles down the stairwell and echoes inside the vault.

"They're playin' my song, Fred. Have we got a deal?"

He stands at the position of attention and pops a salute. "Yes, ma'am."

I run up the stairs, and Alice meets me halfway. "Any luck?"

"Not really. I hate to say it, but I think there's more than one angry spirit in this bank. The sooner we get out of here, the better. Now let's send Jeff out the front and see if Ears came up with the loading order for us."

She grips my arm as though we've been friends since elementary school, and we rush past Queenie, back to the main lobby.

The White Rabbit has the keys out and nods when he sees me. "We put Mr. Curb in his office, and we're about to send out Jeff. I decided you're gonna drive the bus. I don't want to take a chance on that sniper picking off one of my crew once we're through the alley."

"No problem. So what's the order?"

"You first, Hatter's got your back, then it's me, Alice, Smiley, and Queenie bringing up the rear."

"Understood. Do you want me to walk Jeff out, or just open the door for him?"

The White Rabbit strokes his long plastic whiskers and makes a low humming sound. "Go ahead and walk him out. That way, they know you're okay."

"Good plan. Come on, Jeff."

Ears unlocks the door and I reach for my phone. "Almost forgot. I need to let them know we're releasing a hostage." I wipe my hand comically across my brow, and the Mad Hatter chuckles.

Once I've prepped Deputy Paulsen, I push the door open and maneuver Jeff out onto the sidewalk.

The former blabbermouth staggers forward, and, once he stumbles into the street, a deputy from Broken Rock swoops in and escorts him off to the side. I turn and lift the back of my coat in the direction of Deputy Paulsen. I'm not sure whether she sees the gun tucked into my waistband, or what she'll think if she does, but every piece of information could matter.

The door closes, and Ears secures it.

I gesture to the lock. "Good thinking. We don't want them coming in behind us while we're loading onto the bus."

He nods his large ears and drops the ring of keys on a desk. The desk on the opposite side of the lobby from Tilly's. Looking away, I thank the powers that be that no one has noticed that receiver dangling off the side of her desk.

The White Rabbit holds his gun in the air. "Let's move!"

The five of us hustle toward the back door to join Queenie, who's carefully peering through the small crack between the door and the doorjamb.

"What's the story, Queenie?"

"All clear, Ears. The guy who dropped it off exited the alley that way. I didn't see him look up, or make any signals. I think they were telling the truth when they said they pulled back."

"Okay. Lineup."

I take the lead, the Mad Hatter behind me, and so on.

Slowly opening the door, I poke my head out and glance up and down the alley.

Hatter prods me with his shotgun. "Let's go. The longer we wait, the worse it's going to be."

Lurching forward, I head directly to the bus. Classic me, stumbles as I attempt to hustle up the deep steps. My knee bangs sharply into the metal edge and I hiss an unladylike expletive.

The White Rabbit shouts from the back, "What's the holdup?"

I scramble to my feet and slide into the driver's seat. Hatter takes the seat behind me. Alice and the Cheshire Cat head straight to the back, while the

White Rabbit and Queenie hunker down in the aisle about halfway between.

Ears shouts, "Let's go! Get this bus moving!"

I glance at the gas gauge, and can't believe it's full. I really thought Erick would pull a fast one on them, but I guess he didn't want to take any chances with my life. Shifting the beast into drive, I ease down the alley and wonder if anyone's going to take a shot at us.

For a brief moment, I can almost feel Erick's presence but it slips away. I really hope he listened to the dispatch tape. And that he got the clue about Canada. Man, do I want to see him again . . . to kiss his wonderful, pouty lips.

I love you, Erick.

And with that, I turn toward Main Street, head past the newspaper office, and wind my way back toward the scenic highway that encircles our great lake.

Canada, here we come.

CHAPTER 12

THE LUXURY MOTOR coach is easier to drive than I'd feared. My brief experience driving bobtail trucks for the plant nursery back in Arizona has come in handy. And I'm extremely grateful for a bus with an automatic transmission. However, now that we're out on the open road, my thoughts are wandering.

What's going to happen when we approach the Canadian border? If Erick figured out my not-so-subtle code referencing CC, his Canadian Mountie buddy, there's likely to be an armed reception. Since I'm sitting in the front seat, driving the get-away vehicle, there's a higher-than-average chance that their sniper will take me out first.

I've seen the movies. The sniper takes out the driver, the bus swerves, rolls, and skids to a crashing halt just before hitting the law enforcement barricade.

After doing more than my share of stupid things in my life, I've had to face my mortality more than once, but today has a sense of finality I've never felt before.

The energy of the crew is somewhat relaxed, now that we've officially gotten away and are outside the city limits. The Hatter's not even holding his shotgun on me anymore. Even though I knew it wasn't loaded, there's a sense of relief when the boom stick is removed from my right shoulder.

Glancing up into the mirror, I observe the gang. Smiley and Alice are sitting together on the left side of the bus. She has the window seat and has pushed her mask up to get a better view.

She's young. Much younger than I imagined. In fact—my psychic senses flicker back online—she's a minor. Great! Now I'll have to fight between my urge to save her and my need to see justice served. At least I got that gun out of her hands.

Right! I have a loaded gun. I could stop this bus, threaten them with my gun, and run away. Sure, that'd be the thing to do if I was looking to get an award for the world's shortest unsuccessful escape.

There are still three armed robbers on this bus, and my brief relationship with them has definitely taught me that the White Rabbit didn't come to play.

Ears and Queenie still have their disguises on and their guns drawn. Although, the ringleader's hold is way more relaxed than it was in the bank. "Hey, Mitzy?"

"What's up, Doc?"

Queenie and Hatter chuckle at my Bugs Bunny reference.

"You had a solid plan. I'm almost sorry we're going to have to hold you for ransom when we hit Canadian soil."

"Well, you could always let me go, and clear your conscience."

He laughs loudly and adjusts his pistol. "Nah, I don't want your sheriff to think we've gone soft."

At the mention of Erick, my heart sinks. I blew it. I had the world's perfect man, and I chose to keep my secrets rather than trust him fully. Now I'm going to die in a hail of gunfire and never have the opportunity—

The engine sputters. My eyes widen and I look into the mirror.

The White Rabbit is on his feet, walking toward me. "What gives? How much gas we got?"

"It's almost full. I swear. I told you, Erick's a straight shooter."

Before I can continue my defense of the sheriff,

the hairs on the back of my neck blast me with an intense tingle and my mood ring turns to ice as the scene reflected in the giant mirror above my head shifts dramatically.

The floor seems to explode! Carpet flies and metal clangs.

My foot comes off the gas without thinking.

The White Rabbit lurches forward and shouts, "Step on it!"

As though I'm watching an action film, Erick pops up from the floor, grips an open overhead compartment, and swings through the air. He lands two boot-clad feet directly in Queenie's chest as the man in glam attempts to get to his feet.

The Queen of Hearts goes down hard and the White Rabbit pulls his gun.

I can't return fire and drive this thing. But I can drive badly!

Swerving the bus back and forth, I knock Ears off his feet.

The Cheshire Cat shoves Alice into the restroom, pulls his gun, and aims at Erick.

Instinct takes over, and I yell, "Check your six, Sheriff!"

Erick spins and fires a round into Smiley's leg. The Cheshire Cat goes down grinning and drops his gun in the aisle.

The Mad Hatter stands helplessly with his

empty shotgun. But suddenly he's struck with a bolt of bravery. He pushes past Ears and aims the shotgun at the sheriff.

"Red light!" I shout at the top of my lungs and hope Erick has played the game.

He grabs the luggage rack, and I slam on the brakes. The Cheshire Cat's gun slides forward several feet, but not all the way to Erick. Ears and Hatter go down a second time.

The Mad Hatter struggles to get to his feet.

Grabbing the shotgun from Hatter, and using it like a bat, I crack him hard across the side of the head.

I left the bus in drive when I abandoned my post in the driver's seat. It's only idling, but the motor coach inches forward.

As the Hatter tumbles down the stairwell toward the folding door, I flip it open and drop a one-liner even Arnold Schwarzenegger would endorse. Plus, I deliver it in my best Arnold-esque accent, "Looks like this is your stop."

He falls out of the bus, onto the side of the road, and I quickly close the door.

Queenie's wig is askew, and he still hasn't moved.

That leaves an injured cat and an angry rabbit. Not my best day, but at least that evens the odds.

The White Rabbit fires, and Erick jerks backward.

"No!"

I pull the gun from my waistband and fire one into the rabbit's haunch.

When he grips his thigh and goes down, I bring my knee up hard into the side of his head and rip the ears off his murderous body.

He reaches for his fallen pistol. I take aim and shoot at his hand to discourage recovery.

Grabbing his gun, I stumble over him and kick the rabbit's filthy paw off my ankle as I lurch toward Erick.

"Erick! Erick!"

His eyes open, and he lifts his head.

"Don't try to talk. You've been hit. Do you have a radio? I need to call an ambulance."

He makes a fist with his left hand and knocks firmly on his chest. "Ceramic, Moon."

The surge of relief that floods through me is inexplicable. Whatever happens, whatever secrets he needs to know, I'm finally all in. I'm an open book.

As I attempt to embrace Erick, two things happen simultaneously. Someone grips a fistful of my hair, yanks hard, and drags me off Erick.

The Cheshire Cat slinks forward, dragging his injured leg behind.

"Don't move!"

My guns lie on the floor where I dropped them when I fell to my knees beside Erick.

The White Rabbit may not have a gun, but he slips an arm tightly around my throat as he offers his deal. "Drop your gun, Sheriff! You do exactly as I say, or I'll choke the life out of her right before your very eyes." His voice is unwavering, but I can sense the pain he's hiding beneath the surface. He has the upper hand now, but at least I put a bullet in his unlucky rabbit foot—well, leg actually.

Erick drops his gun and gets to his feet with his hands in the air.

I'm such an idiot! We had them on the ropes. My stupid emotions got the better of me. If I'd stayed focused and leaned into my extra senses, I would've known Erick wasn't hurt.

The Cheshire Cat moans loudly as he struggles to his feet and retrieves Erick's weapon. He presses the gun into the sheriff's back.

I don't know exactly how body armor works, but something tells me that a shot from close range is likely to cause some type of injury. Maybe not death, but something bad.

My lungs are screaming for air and things in my peripheral start to get blurry. I don't have a plan, and I'm pretty sure I ruined whatever plan Erick had.

The precise moment I'm about to give up hope,

my natural klutzdom and lack of attention to detail pays off big.

The bus, which has been slowly idling forward, now lurches off the road and plunges into the ditch.

Everything inside the bus goes topsy-turvy. Ears loses his hold on me, and I scramble to put some distance between us as I'm tumbling.

I hope the unexpected lurch is as fortuitous for Erick as it was for me.

Wedged between two of the high-backed seats, I hear a voice that makes everything right in the world.

"Tea party's over. We're all getting off the bus, single file. Mitzy will secure your wrists while I hold the guns."

Un-wedging my rear end from the narrow space between the seats is a daunting task, but eventually I get to my feet—flushed, but alive. Before a satisfied smile can even touch my lips, horror grips my face and nausea turns my stomach.

Alice must've crept out of the bathroom during the last round of shenanigans, and she retrieved Smiley's gun. Her hand is visibly shaking as she aims at Erick. "Look, Sheriff, I don't wanna hurt anyone. Just you and Mitzy get out of the bus. We don't need a hostage anymore. You can get off the bus, and, like, everything will be fine."

Erick doesn't lower his gun, or the pistol he retrieved from the White Rabbit. His eyes dart toward me and I shake my head, "No."

I hope he knows what that means, but, on the off chance that he didn't notice my subtle head movement, or has possibly misinterpreted the signal, I attempt to reach Alice. "Hey, you haven't done anything wrong yet. You didn't take any money at the bank, you didn't hurt anyone, and you actually helped me."

The White Rabbit grumbles. "You helped her, Alice? What the—?"

"Don't listen to him, Alice. You saw what happened at the bank. That ghost was the guy who robbed the bank in the 1970s. He's been haunted by what he did for fifty years. You remember what your Nan said? No unfinished business. Right?"

Her shaky hand lowers the gun a few inches.

I'm getting through. "Alice, if you put your gun down, I know Sheriff Harper will get you the best deal he can. He's fair. I promise you. And I'll pay for a lawyer, if you need one. I'll do whatever it takes. You're too young to ruin your life with one bad decision."

Ears makes a counteroffer. "One bad decision! Who are you kidding? She's been in the crew for over a year. We've knocked off forty-two local banks. There's no way you can prove she had nothing to do with any of this. If we're going down, she's going down."

Erick picks up my torch. "Not necessarily. She doesn't look like the mastermind of this gang. And if she turns state's evidence, I can get her immunity. But you better decide fast, Alice. I've got deputies running a thirty-second delayed pursuit. Once they get here, the deal is off the table."

Alice lowers the gun almost to her side. "What's immunity?"

Dear Lord baby Jesus! She might be younger than I thought. "Alice, immunity means you don't go to jail. You have a second chance. You can make things right."

She doesn't drop the gun, but she slowly collapses onto one of the high-backed luxury seats.

It's over.

I'm alive. Erick's alive.

We captured the gang with no loss of life, and I know how much that last part means to Erick.

## CHAPTER 13

ONCE DEPUTY PAULSEN and the reinforcements arrive, the fear I held at bay for nearly four hours hits me like a tsunami. I thought I could make it to the ambulance, but—

The blue eyes smiling down at me are bursting with unspoken emotions. "Hey, you picked a weird time to take a nap, Moon."

I toy with the idea of faking amnesia—again—but that seems played out. "This is like the third time you've tried to send me off in an ambulance, Sheriff. Are you trying to tell me something?"

He inhales sharply, and his lips are on mine in a flash. "Just that I love you. And I'm glad there were no corpses today."

My heart stutters in my chest as the replay of

the bullet hitting him on the bus plays on repeat inside my head. "Me too. Hey, I need to tell—"

"Sheriff, the minor says she wants to cut a deal. We need you out here." Deputy Paulsen nods once in my direction.

My true confessions to Erick will have to wait. I return Paulsen's nod. When she lay on that icy sidewalk today and begged me to get them to send out her mom—well, that was the closest she's ever come to being human in my presence.

I take the blood pressure cuff off my right arm and assure the paramedic that I'm fine. He shakes his head, but lets me leave.

The scene is finale worthy. The sun is dipping into the west. Pinkish-orange light reflects off the drifting snow and softens the harsh flashing lights of the cruisers and emergency vehicles.

The gang, officially unmasked, stands in handcuffs under the watchful eyes of ten sheriff's deputies.

A tall deputy with intense brown eyes approaches. "Hey, I'm Boomer. You did a heckuva job today. I've seen a few of these hostage situations go south real fast." He offers his hand and I shake it firmly.

"Nice to meet you. I'm Mitzy Moon."

"Oh, trust me, I know. Harper asked me to take you into town. He's got to escort the minor back to the station and get her immunity locked down. He said he'll catch up with you in about an hour." Boomer gestures toward a Broken Rock vehicle.

My gaze lingers on Erick's back, but I know his duty to the citizens comes first. "Sure. Thanks." I wave, but no one sees.

Boomer kindly makes the drive in silence, and I thank him again when he drops me at the bookshop.

Grams is on me the second I crack the door. She's so close it feels a little like possession.

"Oh, Mitzy! Odell told me what happened. I've been frantic." She tries to hug me, but she's too freaked out to have any substance.

"I'm completely knackered. Can you give me some time to shower and get my emotions under control?"

"Knackered, sweetie?" She arches a perfectly drawn brow.

"Is that what I said? Weird. My mom used to say that at the end of a long day. Anyway, I'm gonna hop—let me rephrase—collapse into a steamy shower or maybe a bubbly tub and try to forget everything I ever knew about talking rabbits in Wonderland."

"If you insist, dear."

"I do." Stumbling up the circular staircase, I'm sort of aware of Ghost-ma's continued warnings and concerns, but mostly my brain is trying every trick in the book to forget that gunshot on the bus.

SADLY, MY DREAM of a quiet night confessing my psychic secrets to Erick is not to be. When I hit the medallion of twisted ivy and exhale as the bookcase door slides open—

Half the town is crammed into my bookshop, and Twiggy is passing pizzas around like she hasn't a priceless book care in the world.

All right, I guess this is happening. I dive into the fray and let the hugs and laughter wash away everything the water missed.

Gazing at all the faces of the people I love, crowded into my apartment and spilling onto the Rare Books Loft, my heart feels full. Erick and I have to tell and retell the story of our motor coach adventure until the muscles in my jaw hurt. However, the enthusiasm of our friends and family doesn't wane.

Stellen grabs a fifth slice of pepperoni and pineapple pizza and nudges Erick with his elbow. "Could you hear anything when you were inside that compartment?"

Erick smiles and leans back, resting his elbow on the settee. He's drawing his crowd in and waiting for his moment. "In town, the engine noise and the transmission shifting were pretty much all I could hear. Once Mitzy got the bus on the open road, I could pick up on footsteps and tone of voice. Couldn't really make out any words. But I knew there wasn't much gas in that tank—"

"That's another thing, Sheriff Harper. I was defending you to those crooks all day long! Telling them what a straight shooter you are, and then you sneak in with some underhanded gas tank thinga-majig." Crossing my arms over my chest, I glare up from my seat on the floor and shake my head.

"Hold on. Hold on, Moon. Let's not be getting too high and mighty! You practically joined their gang. Writing up their demands, giving them the idea of a getaway vehicle, and carrying one of their guns!"

The room oohs and aahs in support of the sheriff, and I have to toot my own horn once again.

"Hey, you can't blame me for being persuasive. If it hadn't been for me, none of those hostages would've gotten out of there. And it's not like I gave them a great plan! I was sending them to Canada, for heaven's sake."

Rowdy laughter ripples through the crowd, and Odell raises his glass and calls out from his seat in the loft. "Three cheers to Mitzy Moon, the world's greatest criminal that never was."

Hip hip hooray!

Hip hip hooray!

Hip hip hooray!

I take a drink of my pop, that's right, just plain soda, and wish it were something stronger. But since we have a recovering alcoholic ghost and a couple of minors in our midst, I chose to take the high road.

Plus, I'm thrilled to see Yolo Olson snuggled next to Stellen. The petite, elfin-like creature, with lavender hair, violet eyes, and steampunk attire, has a wholly anime vibe. Luckily, her first year at college hasn't ruined her unique spirit. She's home for spring break and dressed to the nines. The assortment of buckles, straps, and gears connecting her one-of-a-kind garments boggles the mind. Stellen is obviously stoked to have her so near.

I sense my father has something to say, and my chest tightens when I think about how worried he must've been. Before he can make his move, Erick's mother beats him to the punch.

Gracie Harper gets to her feet, grinning like—well, like the Cheshire Cat. "Now, you all might think I'm biased, but I never doubted my Ricky for a second, you know. Ever since he could talk, he's been smart as a whip and twice as fast." She lifts her mug of coffee and beams with a thousand watts of motherly love. "Here's to the best sheriff Pin Cherry Harbor's ever had—remember to vote in

November—and the best son a mother could ever want!"

"Cheers!"

"Hear! Hear!"

Amaryllis and Tally dab at the corners of their eyes, and Grams is full-on ghost sobbing, but luckily I'm the only one who can see that hot mess. Technically, Stellen could see her—but he's only got eyes for one girl in the room.

"Mitzy! I would hardly call it a hot mess to show some genuine emotion. You could've been killed today!"

She sobs anew and swipes at the tears rolling down her cheeks.

Rather than interrupt the festivities, I opt to send Grams a thought message. *Sorry if I scared the resident ghost, Grams. I don't mean to take these risks. Somehow they just find me. And you can show your heartfelt emotions in any way you please. I love you.* And now, I have to wipe a tear from my eye.

Tally grabs her sister's hand and pulls Tilly to her feet. "Well, I'd like to thank Mitzy Moon, Sheriff Harper, and the whole lot of those law enforcement fellas for bringing my sister back to me in one piece."

Tilly curls an arm around her younger sister's shoulder and gives it a squeeze. "Gosh, you know you and Ledo couldn't survive without me."

Tatum raises her glass of cola and beams. "Here's to the best auntie in town!"

Everyone raises their glass, mug, or can, while I succumb to yet another telling of Erick's amazing *Bourne Identity* meets *Speed* meets *Taken* heroics on the bus to nowhere.

Rather than make a public spectacle, my father catches my eye across the room, lifts his glass and winks. We may have only been building a relationship for the last three years, but that tiny gesture speaks volumes to me. He trusts me. He admires me. He's thankful I wasn't hurt, and he'll move heaven and earth to keep things that way.

My brain is exhausted, my psychic powers are fading, and my body actually aches, but I have to take care of some serious supernatural business. A promise is a promise.

Slipping one arm around my kid brother and the other around his on-again-off-again genius girlfriend, I guide them down the curving left balcony of the mezzanine. Once we're out of earshot, I make my ask. "Hey, guys, I need to get the band back together."

For two brainiacs, they're not exactly doing the math. My clever quip is met with dull eyes.

"I have a couple ghosts to dispatch before— I mean, in the next twenty-four hours, and I could use some help."

Yolo bounces on her purple-boot-clad feet and grins. "A ritual?"

Chuckling, I shake my head. "I hope not. These two seem willing enough, but I have to figure out some details of their unfinished business."

Her shoulders sag and her long lashes droop. "Oh, just research then."

I lean in, as though we're in a huddle, and whisper. "We have to solve a nonexistent cold case and trace some crazy genealogy. Who knows what we'll uncover?"

That tidbit brightens her wide, eager eyes, and her happiness is immediately reflected on Stellen's face.

"Are you guys in?"

Stellen places his hand in the center and says, "Ghost Blasters assemble!"

Yolo instantly places her delicate hand on top of his.

However, I'm not convinced. "Ghost Blasters? For real? Is that the best you've got?"

He elbows me sharply. "It's a work in progress. Are you in or not, Mitzy?"

I place one hand under theirs and one on top. "Ghost Blasters for the win!"

We all giggle and throw our stacked hands in the air.

Stellen gets right down to business. "What's our first move?"

"I'll get the case files on the bank robbery that Disco Donnie was involved in—"

Yolo grips my arm and practically glows from the inside out. "Disco Donnie?"

"Not his real name. I'll explain everything tomorrow."

She claps and snickers. "That's lit."

My brother echoes her sentiment. "Yeah, totally lit."

"All right. Tomorrow I'll crack his case wide open, and you two will get all the info you can on Lindy McElroy. Deal?"

"Deal!" they reply in unison.

Turning to rejoin the festivities, I find that the fire of celebration seems to have burned itself out.

The energy of the party is dipping, but before the guests make their exit, Twiggy asks the question on many of our minds. "So what happens to the criminals, Sheriff Harper?"

"Things should be pretty open and shut. Thanks to the friendship Mitzy forged with the seventeen-year-old Alice Cooper." He raises his hand and waves off the questions. "Before anyone asks, it *is* her real name, and she's no relation to the heavy metal performer." Erick shrugs and grins playfully.

A light chuckle passes through the crowd.

"Anyway, she agreed to testify against the others. With her testimony, Mitzy's testimony, and the statements from the rest of the hostages, there isn't a prosecutor in the state who can't win this case. All the money was recovered, and the two injured members of the crew have been treated and released into our custody."

My father initiates a round of applause.

Erick waves for everyone to cease and desist. "I'm grateful things ended as smoothly as they did. Now, I appreciate all the support and the impromptu celebration, but I'm exhausted. So if you don't mind, I think I'm gonna have to call it a night."

You would've thought someone pulled the fire alarm. I've never seen a group of people clear out of an establishment so quickly. Before I can even figure out what's going on, Odell has offered to drive Gracie Harper home, and Grams is promising Erick and me all the privacy we can stand.

Amaryllis offers me a signature bearhug on her way out, and Stellen gives me a friendly punch on the shoulder.

In the span of five minutes, my bookshop goes from a bustling afterparty to an abandoned store.

"Excuse me, Sheriff, did you have some pre-arranged code word? I haven't seen a party clear out that fast since I was in high school and the cops showed up."

Erick grins and nods. "Now, why doesn't that surprise me?"

"Rude." Smiling, I kiss his lips lightly. "But you're not wrong."

He scoops his arms around me and pulls me close. "If loving you is wrong, Mitzy Moon, I don't wanna be right."

Sure, it's cheesy, but when it's whispered directly in your ear by the sexiest lips this side of the Mississippi . . .

Swoon.

## CHAPTER 14

A SOMEWHAT FAMILIAR voice echoes over the intercom and wakes me from a deep slumber. The only words from the early morning message that register in my sluggish grey matter are *chocolate croissants* and *extra-large coffee.*

You don't have to tell me twice. My brain struggles to send the "move" message to my extremities.

"It's not like you to have a wake-up call, Moon."

Yikes! I'm only partially functional. Somewhere in the fog between dreamland and waking, I forgot I wasn't alone. A flicker of guilt hits me. It was too easy to postpone my big secret reveal and lose myself in celebrating Erick being alive last night. One more day couldn't hurt . . .

As I try to slip out of bed, Erick circles his arms around me and nuzzles playfully into my neck. His husky voice makes my skin tingle. "Where do you think you're going?"

"Erick Harper! There are children just outside that door. Get up and make yourself presentable. And . . . act like you slept on the couch."

His laughter fills the room as I rush into the bathroom to splash cold water on my face and drag a comb through my white haystack of a hairdo.

While I'm in the closet selecting today's perfect T-shirt, a fully dressed Sheriff Harper peeks into the room I've nicknamed *Sex and the City* meets *Confessions of a Shopaholic*. His gaze travels around the vast space and stops on the T-shirt in my hands. "*Cute but Psycho*. It's like you have these things custom-made."

I whip the T-shirt at him as though it's a wet towel in a locker room. "Rude!"

He dodges, chuckles, and heads for the door. "But I'm not wrong. If you and your Nancy Drew squad take a break later, let me know. I can meet you at the diner for lunch."

As he reaches toward the medallion that serves as the opening mechanism for the sliding bookcase door, I wave my hands and call out. "Hold on."

Erick turns toward me and grins.

I hustle across the thick carpet and slip into his arms one last time. He leans down and kisses my lips with an intensity that causes my heart to stutter.

"That was—"

He gently strokes the hair back from my face. "Just something to remember me by."

"Yeah, that should do the trick." I swallow and gasp for air.

Sheriff Harper reaches out, presses the plaster circle of twisted ivy, and we wait hand-in-hand as the bookcase slides open.

Yolo and Stellen look up from the table where they've laid out an impromptu breakfast spread.

She winks at me and Stellen blushes a bright fuchsia.

Erick heads across the loft, but before he makes it to the wrought-iron spiral staircase, my brain finally kicks into drive. "Hey, we need the case files for that bank robbery in the '70s. I need to figure out how to get Disco Donnie off the hook."

His brow arches. "Disco Donnie?"

"I'll explain it all later. Can I send Twiggy over to the records office?"

He dips his head in that way that insinuates he's doffing a cap, and smiles. "I'm sure Wayne will be only too happy to hand over whatever she needs."

Ignoring his poke at Twiggy's extracurricular relationship, I calmly reply. "Thank you, Sheriff."

Disappearing down the staircase, his low chuckle echoes softly through the still morning air as he steps out the side door and heads to the station.

Yolo pushes the lovely pink box of pastries toward me and points to one of the large coffees. "I think you only take cream, right?"

"Well remembered."

"I can't really take the credit. Stellen's totally the best brother ever. He knows all kinds of stuff about you."

Since my mouth is already full of chocolate croissant, I'm unable to make a comment. But I shrug and take a long, delicious sip of my black gold.

While I continue to shove flaky treats into my mouth, Stellen makes notes on his phone. "So what's the plan, Mitzy?"

"I'll go over the case files, and you two will head to the library and find out all the deets on Lindy McElroy. I mean, her survivors. We have to figure out this unfinished business and get those earthbound spirits out of the bank today."

Yolo wipes her perfect strawberry mouth with a paper napkin and adjusts her purple, crushed-velvet top hat—complete with steampunk goggles. "If it's a crime scene, isn't it closed for the investigation? How are we gonna get back into the bank?"

I gesture in the direction of my boyfriend's recent exit. "Let me take care of that part. You guys get over to the library as soon as it opens and talk to Pyrrha, the reference librarian. She's well acquainted with Silas and will hopefully be in the mood to do us some favors."

Stellen pushes his bottom lip between his teeth with his finger and bobs his head slowly up and down as he chews his lip. "First, we need to find out the date of the robbery. Then we can find Lindy's obituary. Once we know about the survivors, hopefully we can track one of them down."

I nod my head in agreement. "We know she had a child. Let's hope that child married and had a child of his or her own. If the line ended with Lindy's offspring, we might not be able to get Fred Clements the closure he needs."

"Fred?" Yolo and Stellen question the name in unison.

I give them a crash course on the Pin Cherry Harbor Bank & Trust ghosts as I walk them to the side door. They head out to see what time the library opens, and I place a call to Twiggy. She must be feeling generous after I risked my life attempting to get the drawer money yesterday, because she quickly agrees to stop by and get the files from Wayne. Now I just need to—

"RE-ow." Feed me.

"As you wish, your furry highness." When I turn to make good on my promise, Pye runs in front of me, and plunks into an irritated roadblock position. "What's up, son? I thought you wanted food."

"Ree-oow." A gentle reminder.

"Oh! That's on me. Of course you deserve praise before sustenance." Bending, I scratch his broad head, and he offers me a rare opportunity to stroke his neck below his powerful jaw. I am honored and unnerved. "You tried to warn me about the rabbit robbing the bank and I missed the clue. However, for future reference, Mr. Cuddlekins, a plush toy isn't a great deterrent. Next time try knocking an armed-robbery-themed book off the shelf."

"Ree-OW!" A warning punctuated by a threat.

Pulling my hand back, I swallow loudly. "You're right. I should've made better use of my abilities and figured out the helpful clue. It's all on me."

He squeezes his eyelids closed, over his all-knowing golden eyes, and I swear he's grinning.

While I'm feeding Pyewacket his favorite sugary children's cereal, Grams floats into the back room, carrying a list in her ethereal hands.

"What's that, Grams?"

My voice seems to break her out of a trance and

all color fades from her image. For the first time since I met her, she turns white as a ghost.

Ghost-ma's surprise is immediately replaced with giggles. "Oh Mitzy, you're such a hoot! White as a ghost." Her laughter tinkles like fairy bells.

"No thought-dropping, Isadora. What's that piece of paper in your hand?"

Guilt quickly replaces surprise. "This? It's nothing. I must've left something in the—" Without finishing her sentence, she vanishes through the wall. Paper and all!

"Now that's definitely new." If she'd stuck around for a minute, I could've asked her about the robbery, but the less time I spend around her, the better. I can only get away with the "blank mind" trick for so long. Eventually, I'll mess up and she'll discover I'm onto her big plans. The last thing I want to do is ruin all her hard work. I mean, the hard work of her minions!

Drifting up to the loft, I run through my flimsy plan. If there's any trace of Lindy McElroy, my junior super sleuths will find it. Stretching my arms wide as I yawn, it's hard to ignore how much I've come to rely on friends and family. Something I never thought I'd have the chance to do. When I was bouncing between foster homes, mourning the loss of my beautiful mother, I never imagined relying on anyone. Every time I had to defend myself or run from trouble, I was alone. Me against the world. That's how I thought it would always be. Ever since I arrived in almost-Canada, the universe has tossed me one surprise after another.

Despite all the good things happening in my life, there's a deep dark part of me that worries it's all too perfect. That shattered eleven-year-old girl that had to face life without a mother is still waiting for the other shoe to drop. Why do I have such a hard time believing I deserve good things?

SLAM!

The heavy metal door from the alley bangs closed and startles me from my reverie.

"You gonna come down and get your box of goodies, kid? Or are you waiting for an engraved invitation?" Twiggy's cackle bounces off the tin-plated ceiling and puts me in my place.

"Coming!" I circle down the steps, climb over the "No Admittance" chain hooked at the bottom, and nearly make a clean break. My toe catches and throws me off balance. As I hop forward, flailing my arms like a windup bathtub toy, Twiggy drops the box at my feet and slaps her hand on her dungarees. "Never gets old. I keep thinking it will, but it never does." And with that, she turns and heads into the back room.

I catch myself on the end of the bookcase just in time. "Thanks, I think."

She calls out from the back, "I should be the one thanking you."

"True." After a quick time-space calculation, I have to ask, "Hey, how did you get this evidence so fast?"

There's a sinister chuckle, followed by a vague explanation. "Let's just say I happened to be 'in the room' when Wayne got the call from the sheriff this morning. Wayne offered me a ride to work, and when you called me, we made a little stop on the way."

"Must be nice to be dating a guy with connections."

"Says the gal dating the sheriff." She guffaws at her own joke while I scoop up the evidence box and head upstairs.

Inside the apartment, I clear the coffee table and start reviewing Donnie's case.

A two-page police report.

Three witness statements—all equally vague.

Three confessions that name Donald Whitely as the leader of the gang and mastermind of the robbery.

Then the final nail in the coffin. Tiny Tim's confession. He claims to have tried to stop Donnie from shooting the innocent civilians, but he was too late. Tim blamed both murders on Donnie.

It really was open and shut. My dad's case was

eighteen or nineteen years old when I started digging through it, and we had five boxes of evidence. One box, even for such an old case, seems a little slim.

Clearly, the cops simply recorded exactly what they were told, pinned the murders on Donnie, and the rest of the crew got off easy.

Tim Rosacker, a.k.a. Tiny Tim, served almost five years, but that was the longest sentence by far. The names of the other gang members mean nothing to me. Donnie didn't mention them in his story, and, as far as I know, they only played a part in the armed robbery.

Opening the notes app on my phone, I type up a list of their names. Adding Tim Rosacker at the end, the hairs on the back of my neck tingle and my mood ring burns when I type his alias.

The image in the smoky mists of my antique mood ring shows a baby. I'm not sure what that—

Tiny? Baby?

He was the youngest!

I'm already dialing Erick as the thoughts tumble through my brain. If there's a chance any of these guys are alive—

"What's up, Moon?"

"I'm going through the files from that bank robbery case. Can you run the names of the other guys in the crew and tell me who's still kicking?"

"Sure. Shoot."

We run down the names, and the first three are deceased. Two were repeat offenders who died in prison, and one died of a heart attack eight years ago.

"The last name on the list is Timothy Rosacker. What have you got?"

There's a pause while Erick types the query into his database, and I dig through the remaining contents of the box. We seem to discover our leads simultaneously.

He enthusiastically calls out, "Rosacker's alive." While I shout, "The guns!"

Erick's voice tightens with concern. "What guns? Does someone have a gun? Are you—?"

My brain finally acknowledges the convict update. "Wait, did you say he's alive? Tiny Tim? Where?"

There's a strange pause, and the sheriff seems to be waiting for something.

"Oh, sorry. I found the guns in two evidence bags at the bottom of the box. But you go first."

"Tiny Tim lives in Gooseberry Falls, in an assisted living facility."

"Erick, I need you to dust this gun for prints—actually, both of the guns."

"What are you hoping to find?"

He didn't say no. Let's all remember that. "I'm

hoping that Tim Rosacker's prints are on his gun. If Donnie's story is true, and Tim placed the second gun in his left hand as Donnie was dying, then Tim didn't have time to re-fire it. There's no evidence in the file that indicates anyone checked Donnie for gunshot residue."

"They had a dead bank robber with two guns in his hands and a local young mother murdered in the prime of her life. There had to be a lot of pressure to close the case fast. I don't think anyone did any investigating above and beyond."

"I understand, Erick. But I'm hoping Tiny Tim's print is still on the trigger."

"Drop those evidence bags in your purse and meet me at the diner for brunch."

"Copy that. But you know I don't carry a purse, right?"

He chuckles. "I'm sure you can find something in that endless closet of yours."

"Touché. I'll text the B-team and see if they have anything."

I can't risk losing one of Grams' vintage bags at the crime lab, so I grab a black paper bag with a gold ribbon from the bookshop and drop both guns inside.

Slipping the loaded bag over one arm, I text Yolo and Stellen as I walk toward the diner. Their reply pings back:

"might have something big 👍 no time 4 food"

I keep my response short and sweet. "No problem."

As I slide my phone into my pocket, I can't help but finish the text—in my mind: that means more Sheriff Too-Hot-To-Handle for me.

CHAPTER 15

ERICK DEFINITELY HAD a few minutes head start, because as soon as I walk through the door, Odell strides out of the kitchen with two breakfasts and meets me at the table. "Good morning, Mitzy. Robbed any banks lately?"

"Hilarious, Gramps. Not yet, but the day is young." Ever since I discovered he's my biological grandfather, I've been mentioning it every chance I get.

He chuckles under his breath and slides the food onto the table. Erick offers me a welcoming smile as Odell glances at the gift bag in my hand. "Who's the present for?"

A sly smile creeps across my face as I lean the bag toward him and open it wide.

Surprise grips his lined face, but only for a second. The shock evaporates, and he places a weathered hand on my shoulder. "Have I told you how happy I am to know you're working for the good guys?"

Pushing the bag of weapons toward the sheriff, I pat Odell's hand. "You don't have to thank me, Gramps."

He shakes his head and mumbles, "That never gets old." He raps his knuckles twice on the silver-flecked white Formica and disappears into the kitchen.

Erick is working on a large bite of blueberry pancakes, but pauses to peek into the bag. "What are we going to do if we find this Tiny Tim's print on the other gun?"

"Hey, it's my job to get ahead of the investigation, not yours."

He nods and licks a drop of syrup from his lip.

What I wouldn't give to be that syrup. Memories of his passionate kiss this morning draw me into my inner world of daydreams.

"Mitzy? Oh, Mitzy Moon. Did I lose you?"

"What? I wasn't doing anything."

His blue eyes sparkle, but he lets me off the hook with a subject change. "Seems like you're pushing for a field trip."

After shoving some perfectly browned home fries into my mouth and washing them down with my favorite go-go juice, I wipe the corners of my mouth like a dainty princess. "I was hoping I could come to the lab with you. That way, *when* we find the fingerprint, we can head straight to Gooseberry Falls." I smile invitingly and bat my eyelashes.

"Wow. You're really laying it on thick. Why is it so important to deal with these ghosts today? They've been in the bank for over fifty years. Why can't they just stay there, like your grandma at the bookstore?"

"I'm glad you asked that, Sheriff. I can honestly say I don't know. Fred Clements may remain timid, but something about spirits bound to this plane, against their will, being prone to dark rages bothers me. Plus, there's the fact that I gave Disco Donnie my word." Taking a hesitant sip of my coffee, I wait for Erick's comment. None arrives, so I up the ante. "Plus, Donnie said if I didn't keep my word, he'd make sure Tilly paid for it. He may be remorseful about what he did back in the '70s, but I definitely don't want to put Tilly in the ghost crosshairs of a known murderer."

Erick finishes his breakfast, takes a long sip of coffee, and carefully wipes his mouth. "Then I suppose the mountain of paperwork on my desk will have to wait. And what story will I be giving my deputies—assuming we find what we need, and I have to escort you into the bank later today?"

"Well, I think we've used the one about how it helps me remember the sequence of events if I can be inside the venue—or something like that. If it ain't broke, don't fix it."

He shakes his head, and his shoulders slump in defeat. "At your service, Miss Moon."

It doesn't take me long to power through the rest of my breakfast. I bus our dishes and accept a thank-you hug from Tally.

"Ledo said to tell you he was sorry he couldn't make it to the celebration last night. He had an emergency surgery on a guinea pig. But he wanted me to tell you he's glad you're all right."

"No worries. There were too many people as it was—but it was really nice of everyone. Tell him thanks for me." Good save, if I do say so myself.

Tally smiles brightly and nods. Heading toward the door, I sigh with satisfaction and wave to Odell.

Erick hurries ahead to leave instructions for his deputies while I wait by the car with my sack of pistols.

Sheriff Harper opens the passenger door on his cruiser for me. I drop onto the seat and ogle him as he walks around to the driver's side.

It's a short ride, and I'm too full to make conversation.

The lab has significantly tighter security than

the sheriff's station. I have to sign in, show my driver's license—

"You still have your Arizona driver's license?"

I gaze up at Erick like he's crazy. "Of course. It doesn't expire for like thirty years. Why would I get a new one?"

"Because you don't live in Arizona anymore."

"Sure, but I'm still in the United States of America, right? I'm a licensed driver in one of those 'united' states. My license is valid."

He reaches out and takes the license from the clerk when she returns from the copy machine. "I'll be hanging onto this, Moon. In exchange for these series of favors, I'll expect you to get a proper driver's license."

I'm in no position to argue with the man holding my permission to drive. However, I withhold verbal agreement and glare at him instead.

The clerk slides a visitor badge through the curved opening at the bottom of the window. I accept it and clip it to my T-shirt.

Erick leads the way to the lab, and a young redhead in a lab technician's coat smiles broadly when she sees him. "Sheriff Harper! Great to see you. Glad I'm working today. How can I help you?"

Easy, girl. This man's spoken for. I'd hate to have to body slam her before she tests these guns for prints.

"Roxy, I'd like you to meet Mitzy Moon. She's assisting the department on a case."

She offers her hand, but I'm still having a little pout, so I respond with a curt nod and a plastic smile.

Her arm drops to her side as Erick reaches into my gift bag and extracts the two firearms. "I need you to dust both of these guns for prints."

She picks up a tray and places both bagged guns on it. "A Colt Super .38 and a Saturday night special, or MP-25, if I'm not mistaken."

Erick smiles warmly. "You know your guns, Roxy."

Her cheeks pinken, and she stares at the tray. "Looking for anything in particular?"

He shakes his head. "I'd rather you take your best pass and see what you get. I trust your instincts."

Oh, he trusts *Roxy's* instincts, does he? Meanwhile, he's nailing me to the wall for every hunch I get. I'm definitely gonna be waiting in the parking lot for this chick.

"Hey, is something wrong?" Erick places a hand on my shoulder.

"No. Why?" My eyes dart toward the floor.

"That look on your face—"

"Oh, it's nothing. I was thinking about something else."

He lifts an eyebrow and nods in a way that says he's not buying what I'm selling.

Despite her unnecessary overtures toward my sheriff, even I have to admit that Roxy has got skills. She's processed both guns and uploaded two sets of fingerprints to check against the AFIS database in less than twenty minutes.

Pin Cherry Harbor may be the town that tech forgot, but this lab makes up for all those deficiencies. Erick and I stand behind the tech as she tags the loops and whorls. While the computer searches for matching markers, she returns to her work area and picks up a clipboard. "Sheriff Harper, what case am I billing this to?"

I hope my gulp isn't audible.

Sometimes I forget what a cool customer Erick can be. "Let's bill it to community service, Roxy. This legwork ties into a cold case that hasn't officially been reopened."

She smiles and winks as she makes a note on her clipboard.

A wink? Oh man, I'm definitely going to have to do something about this. "Erick, did you say you're bringing dinner to my place tonight?"

That got her attention. Her ink pen stutters to a stop on her little form and my psychic senses detect she's holding her breath.

Erick leans back and scrunches up his face.

"Did I say that? Man, I must've been high on blueberry pancakes. I don't remember that. But I'm happy to pick up whatever you want. Angelo and Vinci's? Or are you in the mood for Chinese?"

Bless his innocent little heart. He has no idea there's a Battle Royale happening right in front of him. However, I'm not going to miss my opportunity to land the killing blow. I slip my arm through his and lean toward him with a cheesy smile. "Why don't you surprise me? You know what I like."

Roxy drops her pen.

My gentleman of a boyfriend moves to retrieve it, but I manage to get one of my sturdy hips in the way—accidentally.

She picks up her own pen and finally returns to the computer. "I'm afraid nothing is coming up as a match in AFIS. There was one set of prints on the Colt Super .38, and the same palm print was on the Saturday night special."

Erick extracts himself from my needy grasp and steps toward the screen. "What about the other set?"

"Same result. No match. The other set of prints was only on the Saturday night special. Specifically, the magazine release and the trigger. Any other prints were obscured by the smudged palmprint."

Now she has my attention. "Did you say the trigger?"

"That's correct. There was only one print there. And it was not a match for the prints on the Colt Super .38."

Bingo. Yahtzee. Full House. That proves Donnie was telling the truth. "Why aren't the prints coming up? We know the suspects were involved in a robbery."

Erick intervenes. "AFIS was established in the '90s. Tim Rosacker must have gone straight before that, which means his prints were never uploaded. Sorry, Mitzy. Looks like a bust."

I place a hand on my hip and widen my eyes. "Not entirely. It just means we have to make the drive to Gooseberry Falls."

There's a strange sense of satisfaction emanating from Roxy. She must assume we're fighting. Poor woman. She has no idea how our relationship works.

"Thanks for getting this processed so quickly, Roxy. You're definitely one of the best techs we've got."

Her zeal returns, and her whole face lights up with a smile. "Thanks, Sheriff Harper." She returns the guns to the evidence bags and Erick puts them in my flimsy gift bag.

We say our goodbyes and head out to the patrol car. No sooner has he started the engine than he launches into an inquest of his own. "So, was that a catfight I just witnessed?"

"I'm sure I have no idea what you're talking about." I cross my arms and stare out the passenger window.

"Okay. It seemed like you were eager to let Roxy know about our relationship, even though you usually have a thing about public displays of affection."

I have a thing? The nerve of this guy. "Fine. I didn't like the way you were calling her *Roxy* and talking about how you trust her instincts. I never get anything but grief from you about my hunches."

His smile falters. "Former Deputy Roxborough is happily married. You've got nothing to worry about. She worked with us for about six months and picked up the nickname before she got accepted to medical school and took the ME track. She's just friendly and good at her job. And as far as your hunches go—"

"Never mind."

He reaches across and places a hand on my knee. "There's more to your hunches than instinct, Mitzy. We both know that."

My post-ordeal guilt has lessened. If he thinks he's going to trick me into having this discussion in the middle of an investigation, he's wrong. Time for a classic left-field question. "If it turns out that Tiny

Tim is the one who actually killed Lindy McElroy, are you going to make an arrest?"

He withdraws his hand, and my extra senses feel a subtle energetic wall rise between us. "I'm not sure. As of right now, we don't have much to go on. A ghost story and a fingerprint that doesn't match anything in the database."

We make the rest of the drive in silence, and when we walk into the facility in Gooseberry Falls, a quick flash of Erick's badge provides instant access to Tim Rosacker's room.

As we head down the hall, the nurse mentions Tim is suffering from lung cancer and other complications resulting from a lifelong smoking habit. She pushes open the pale-peach door and gestures toward the occupant.

The elderly man hunched over in his easy chair hardly looks like a murderer. However, I believe Donnie's story. The only thing left to do now is figure out a way to make Tim Rosacker confirm those details.

## CHAPTER 16

THE MAN SLUMPED before us may bear no resemblance to my fantasy image of the infamous Tiny Tim, but that doesn't stop his old heart from racing when he catches sight of Erick's uniform. "What can I do for you, Officer?"

"It's sheriff. Sheriff Harper. My friend and I just came to chat with you. I hope that's all right?"

Erick offers me the chair opposite Tim, as he casually stands and introduces me. "This is Mitzy Moon. She owns a bookstore in the town of Pin Cherry Harbor. Have you heard of it?"

Tim shakes his head no, but the spike in his pulse and the rapid breathing say otherwise.

I need to build some rapport with this man before I hit him with my questions about Lindy McElroy's murder. Perhaps a loose link to his past will do the trick. "I'm Shelly's great-granddaughter. You might've known Shelly."

His foggy eyes lock onto me with crisp clarity. "Shelly and I never had any daughters, granddaughters, or great-granddaughters. She had a stroke and died nine years ago. I don't know what you're playing at, but I'm not interested." He reaches toward the call button with his right pointer finger, and my psychic senses kick into hyperdrive.

I strike like a cobra, and grab the remote from his chair, careful to put my fingers on the sides and avoid the buttons. "Erick, pull a print off this." It's a total bluff, but I hope my whip-smart boyfriend can play along.

Tim attempts to rise from his chair, but I lift my hands and wave him back. "Look, Tiny Tim, I tried to do this the easy way, but it looks like that's not your style."

At the use of his old gang handle, Tim's entire energy shifts from doddering old man to defensive, dangerous murderer in hiding. "Who sent you?" His voice has the rasp of illness and the chill of fear.

"We'll get to that. What I'd like to know is how you ended up marrying Donnie's old lady?"

At the mention of his dead friend, Tim's eyes widen. "Who are you?"

"You answer my question, and I'll answer yours." I lean back in my chair and cross my arms.

Tim's mouth works back and forth for a few moments while he considers my offer. Lucky for me, he bites. "Shelly was real upset after that cop whacked Donnie. I was there for her, you know?" He coughs and pats his chest.

I nod.

"One thing led to another. It was all innocent enough."

"So you're telling me that framing your best friend for murder, and blaming an entire bank robbery on him, is innocent?"

Tim narrows his gaze. "Your turn."

"Fair enough." Taking a deep breath, I launch into my tale. I choose to go with the idea that I'm a medium that happened to bump into Donnie's ghost while conducting business at the bank. No need to drag out the whole botched robbery story.

Tim leans forward, one gnarled hand grasping the other. "You expect me to believe you were talking to Donnie's ghost? Get outta here."

"I'm not leaving until I get what I came for, Tiny Tim. I know that security guard was going to shoot you. He hesitated, and that gave you the opportunity to kill Lindy McElroy. The guard went down, and he got one shot off. His crazy shot missed you and nicked Donnie's femoral artery. As your friend bled out in the middle of that bank, you pressed your gun into his left hand."

Tim's eyes grow wider with each sentence.

"Then you and your crew walked out of there, called Donnie the ringleader, and let him take the rap for two murders. How am I doing so far?"

A deep cough rattles his chest. He shakes his shoulders and wrings his hands. "It's what we talked about. Everyone knew the drill. Donnie shoulda made his shot count. It's not my fault that guard got one off before his ticker stopped."

"Maybe not. But it is your fault Lindy McElroy is dead. Leaving her child motherless. That is your fault."

Tim leans back in his chair and hangs his head. The fog creeps back over his eyes and I can sense that he's lost in a memory. Good. Let him play through that scene in his mind a few times.

I'm sure his confession will never be admissible in court, but I need to hear him say it nonetheless. Picking up his apple juice, I trace the truth runes Silas taught me into the liquid. "Here, Mr. Rosacker, maybe this will help that cough."

His hands shake as he places the straw between his lips, but he takes a long pull of the liquid.

I set the cup back on the tray beside him and glance toward Erick.

He's tapping out a text on his phone, and I wait for him to finish.

"Erick, were you able to send a photo of the print to Roxy?"

He looks at me, arches an eyebrow, and picks up the call button remote. As he wiggles it back and forth it all clicks into place, and he grins with satisfaction.

Before he says anything, I know I'm on the right track. "Sheriff, can you read him his rights and record his confession?"

Erick walks hesitantly toward Tim. "What makes you think he's going to confess?"

As much as I hate to say it . . . "It's a hunch."

Sheriff Harper informs Tim Rosacker of his Miranda rights and presses record on his phone.

Now it's my turn to finish what I started. "Tim Rosacker, a.k.a. Tiny Tim, what role did you play in the bank robbery that ended in the death of Lindy McElroy?"

Tim turns toward me, and I can feel the struggle within him.

"State your name for the record." I point toward the recording device in Erick's hand.

"Timothy Ernest Rosacker."

"Were you involved in the robbery at the Pin Cherry Harbor Bank & Trust in 1975?"

"Yes, I was." He presses a rheumatoid arthritis crippled hand to his throat and his eyes dart left and right.

"Please walk me through the events of that day."

Tim attempts to circumvent the scene I'm most interested in by supplying tons of unnecessary details leading up to the robbery.

"Tell me about the woman who kept mentioning her child."

He struggles to press his lips together, but the alchemy has done its work. "There was this broad. She kept going on about her kid. We were almost clear when Lumpy said the cops were on the move."

"And what happened next?"

"We needed to get the cash from the vault. Everyone just had to sit tight for a few more minutes. Two of the guys were taking the rent-a-cop downstairs, and that dumb chick made a break for it." His hands clench into weak fists.

"This would be the woman you came to know was Lindy McElroy?" Erick's voice surprises me, but I understand his need to establish the correct identity of the victim.

Tim nods. "Yeah, that's what they said in court."

Erick moves the recording device closer to Tim. "Did you shoot Lindy McElroy, Mr. Rosacker?"

His swollen knuckles whiten, but the runes

compel him. "Yeah. Yeah, I did. All right? She was going to mess everything up."

Erick glances toward me and continues. "And then what happened?"

"Donnie fired one into the guard, and the guard went down. The gunshot scared me and I fired at the broad."

"You mean, Mrs. McElroy?"

"Yeah, McElroy." His voice is soft and almost remorseful. "But like she said"—he gestures toward me—"the cop got one off. He hit Donnie real bad." Tim gazes out the window and continues. "I ran over to him, you know? I tried to get him up, but he was bleeding so much. He said he wasn't gonna make it. He said we should go with the plan."

Uncrossing my arms, I angle toward him. "So instead of applying pressure to your friend's wound and waiting for help to arrive, what did you do?"

"I shoved my gun into his left hand. His lights were going out. We had to stick to the plan."

Erick finishes the interrogation with one final question. "Mr. Rosacker, is it your testimony that you killed Lindy McElroy and placed your MP-25, also known as a Saturday night special, into Donald Whitely's left hand?"

Tim drops his head into his hands and rubs his face. "Yeah, I did it. I shot the lady, and I set up my buddy. I did it all." He leans back in his seat and moans. "But I learned my lesson. I went straight. I took care of Shelly and the boys, and I never put my toe over the line again."

Erick stops the recording on his phone and sighs heavily. "I don't think Lindy McElroy's widower or her child would find much comfort in those words."

I recognize a good exit line when I hear one. So, despite my lingering curiosity, I get to my feet and follow Erick out of the small room, which is somehow drab and cheery at the same time.

The road to Pin Cherry unfolds ahead of us. "So what happens next, Sheriff?"

He twists his hands on the steering wheel and sighs. "I'll take the confession and the fingerprint evidence to the district attorney, but without a pressing need to reopen such an old case, I'm not sure they'll make a move on Mr. Rosacker."

"Well, I think it sucks that he got away with murder."

Erick takes his eyes off the road for a moment and gazes at me. There's a deep sadness swirled with compassion. "You saw him, Mitzy. He's a broken man. He lost everything he ever cared about and is being consumed by a disease of his own making. There may not be a murder conviction on his record, but he's definitely serving a life sentence."

I can't argue with that. Erick is a lawman, but he leads with his heart, not his gun.

He reaches across and rubs his hand on my knee. "What about your side of things?"

"My side of things? What do you mean?"

Erick chuckles for the first time on the return drive. "The ghost side."

"Oh, that! I'll tell Donnie about the fingerprint and play the confession for him. If that doesn't take care of his unfinished business, I don't know what will."

"What about the other one? The security guard."

"Hmmmm. I better check in on the junior sleuths. I'm hoping they've come up with something I can use on that front." Sliding my phone from my pocket, I fire a text off to Stellen and Yolo.

There's no response.

I know for a fact that humans their age are never without their cell phones. Maybe they have their phones silenced since they spent the day in a library. Quickly swiping to my speed dial list, I tap Stellen's name.

He answers on the first ring, but his voice is hushed.

Before I can ask any of my pressing questions, he offers me a vague stall tactic and promises more when he sees me at the bookshop.

Erick's voice is filled with concern. "That didn't exactly sound good. Are the kids okay?"

"Stellen was being super sketchy. He said what they found is bigger than any of us could've imagined. They're waiting at the bookstore, so I guess we'll find out in a few minutes."

The sheriff swallows up several miles of the road in silence. "Then what?"

"Assuming what they found is useful, we'll need access to the bank tonight. I want to get this ghost business handled ASAP. I don't want any of this weird energy hanging around on my birthday."

There's a pulse of nervous excitement from the driver's seat, and I quickly prepare to hide my knowledge of the surprise party.

"That's the first time I heard you mention your birthday this whole week. Do you have plans with your family?"

Here goes nothing. "Nothing official. I mean, I'm not even used to celebrating, you know? I'm sure Amaryllis will make a cake, but other than that, it should be pretty casual."

Laughter erupts from his throat, and he steadies himself on the steering wheel as he catches his breath. "If there's any way you can carve out an hour or two for your current boyfriend, amidst those casual plans, I'd appreciate it."

Stealing a quick glance at his smug expression, I can tell he's mostly fooled by my performance. "Sure. Shouldn't be a problem."

The sparse lights of Pin Cherry loom into view, and within minutes we're parked in the cul-de-sac at the end of Main Street.

I'm pleased I chose to wear my special key today. As we approach the front door, I pull the chain from around my neck and hold the large brass key, with its unique triangle-shaped barrel, in my hand. One more of the special things that link me, inseparably, to this town.

Pushing the key into the lock, I twist it three times and feel the door and the store beyond opening. Even though Stellen let himself in through the side door, the bookstore isn't officially "open" until I unlock this portal.

Thundering footsteps greet us. Stellen is in the lead, and Yolo lags, lost in thought.

"Hey, guys, what did you find? I can't believe you are being so mysterious."

Stellen grabs my arm and tugs me forward. "Come on. I'm going to let her tell you."

Erick steps into the circle and Yolo bounces on her toes as she adjusts the lapel of her deep-brown brocade waistcoat. "I'll start at the beginning. That's the only way any of it will make sense."

We nod, and she continues.

"Lindy McElroy was survived by her husband and three-year-old daughter, Rosa. Lindy's husband died less than a year later, and Rosa ended up in foster care."

A stabbing pain hits my heart. At least I was eleven when I got dropped into the system. I could speak and ask questions. A three-year-old. How awful.

Yolo continues. "We lost the trail for a bit after that. But Pyrrha was totally on it. She knew about a church that helped with a lot of placements at that time. That contact turned us on to some records that led us to Rosa's placement. She was eventually adopted, and the new family kept her name."

I place a hand on her shoulder and give her an encouraging squeeze. "That's good."

"Yeah, but Rosa was uber troubled and had some run-ins with the law. She ended up pregnant at sixteen and—" Yolo tears up, but her perfect eye makeup withstands the salty drops. "—Rosa died in childbirth. I guess the family was, like, totally ashamed, and they gave the baby up for adoption. We had to go over to City Hall to find the name of that baby, but Pyrrha and the city clerk are Bunco pals, so she was really helpful."

Shaking my head, I offer up my amazement. "You guys must have been working some kind of magic. I've never seen the city clerk be helpful to anyone!"

Yolo nods and bounces on her toes again. "So

the baby's name was Emily, and—" She reaches out, squeezes Stellen's arm, and nods for him to pick up the story.

He rubs her hand and takes up the tale. "It seems like bad luck just ran in the family. Emily also got pregnant at sixteen, and she abandoned her baby on the steps of the Lutheran Church."

Erick groans and crosses his arms. "I wish we had better support for people who find themselves in these terrible situations."

Rubbing my hand on his arm, I nod my agreement. "So, is that where the trail ends?"

Yolo regains her composure and picks up the story. "The pastor at the church had been counseling a couple who'd suffered a recent miscarriage. He knew how badly they wanted a child, and he held a lot of sway over social services, because of the many placements credited to his church."

My psychic senses flutter and the mood ring on my left hand burns. It takes all the willpower I don't have to resist spoiling the end of Yolo's tale.

She grabs Stellen's hand for courage and finishes. "There was a note in the basket. The baby's name was Yolonda McElroy. Last year, right after I graduated, my parents told me the story of how I'd been abandoned on the steps of the church. Before that, I never knew I was adopted. Maybe I might have suspected, but I never knew. They thought it was the right time to tell me. And now—"

I wrap my arms around her and squeeze. "I'm so glad the Olson's adopted you, Yolo. Their love broke your family's curse. You're brilliant, and you're gonna achieve amazing things. I'm so happy you were home for this case."

She cries into my shoulder and squeezes me hard. "Me too. Me and Bricklin will be indebted to you forever."

Loosening my arms, I tilt her back and stare down into her tiny pixie face. I can't help but love her like a little sister. "You and your adorable dog don't owe me anything! As far as I'm concerned, you're part of the family. We take care of each other."

Erick pulls us all into a group hug before getting our mission back on track. "Sounds like we have everything we need to take care of these ghosts. I'm no expert, but should we head over to the bank, Mitzy?"

"Yeah. Ghost Blasters assemble."

Stellen laughs and shakes his head. "On second thought, that's not a great name. We're not really blasting anything. We're kinda sending them where they're supposed to be, right?"

Yolo and I nod in unison. She offers her suggestion. "What about Spirit Senders?"

Chewing the inside of my cheek, I nod once. "I think you guys are on the right track. Maybe Ghost Questers?"

That name brings a hearty round of laughter.

"How about we table the naming decision until after we complete this mission?" Erick gestures toward the front door, and none of us argue.

As we reach the exit, a shimmering glow approaches. Stellen and I turn.

Grams sparkles into being and places an ethereal hand on each of our shoulders. "Good luck, Ghost Guides."

Grams for the win.

## CHAPTER 17

ERICK MARCHES UP MAIN STREET to retrieve a key to the bank, while the three Ghost Guides slink down the alley and wait at the rear door. Even though Yolo can't see ghosts, she's an honorary member on account of the séance she took part in—but that's another story.

Excitement hums in the air like electricity down a power line. By the time the sheriff arrives, Stellen and Yolo are beside themselves.

Sheriff Harper slips the key in the lock, but before he opens the door, he turns toward us. "You guys made a believer out of me with the whole ghost of Isadora thing, but this is my first time taking part in a send-off. I'm officially putting Mitzy in charge, but if things take a bad turn, I'm getting all of you out of there whether this ghost business is finished or not. Understood?"

"Copy that." His total "dad" vibe is kind of adorable.

Stellen and Yolo mumble their acceptance, but it's easy to tell that they're in it to win it.

We step inside the bank, and Erick moves toward a light switch. I grab his hand. "It's better if we leave the lights off. Use a flashlight if you have to, but I think there's enough light from the security fixtures and the exit sign."

"10-4."

We make our way to the lobby, and I motion for everyone to sit in a circle on the floor. "Donnie? Donnie, it's Mitzy. I kept my promise."

The first apparition to appear is Fred Clements. His aura has grown a little brighter than it was during the robbery, and I'm sure it has something to do with the faint hope he now carries.

Stellen points, and Yolo and Erick turn to stare at the empty air.

Taking my job as an afterlife interpreter seriously, I take the lead. "Fred, can you find Donnie for me? I think he's going to be happy to hear what I found."

The security guard nods solemnly, and his ethereal shoulders sag.

"Don't worry, Fred, I didn't forget about you.

I'm saving the best for last."

He glows brightly and vanishes.

Erick looks at me and shrugs.

"Fred Clements went to find Donnie. It seems like we need to take care of Disco Donnie's business first. I'm no expert, but that's what feels right."

My supportive boyfriend reaches over and squeezes my hand. "Then I'm sure it is."

Whatever else happens tonight, I have to admire the willingness of this logical military man. He was unceremoniously dumped into the world of the paranormal, and he's done a heckuva job playing catch up. Maybe he could handle the rest of my story—

"Mitzy! So you're more than just a stone cold fox, eh?"

Stellen's eyes widen. He can see ghosts, but he can't hear them. However, with Disco Donnie, a visual is all you need. My stepbrother looks at me and grins from ear to ear.

"Let me make some introductions. Donnie, this is Sheriff Erick Harper, Stellen Jablonski, and Yolo Olson. Everyone, meet Donnie."

He moves around the circle, patting everyone on the shoulder with his shimmering hand. Yolo and Erick jump significantly, but Stellen gives Donnie a big thumbs up when he reaches the end of the circle.

Donnie floats upward, adjusts his huge collar, and shakes a finger at me. "You didn't tell me the kid sees ghosts. Can he hear me too?"

"No, Stellen sees ghosts, but doesn't hear them —yet. Who knows what will happen with practice?"

Donnie slides a thumb along his chin. "That's right. I like your attitude, babe."

"Let's get down to business, Donnie. I promised you I'd get to the bottom of things and help you finish your unfinished business."

He sinks toward the ground, and it almost looks as though his platform shoes are touching the floor. "Yeah, chicks say a lot of things. Did you really come up with anything?"

"This chick doesn't make promises she can't keep, Donnie."

The unnecessary chuckle from the sheriff to my right will have to be ignored, for now.

"I pulled the old case files, and the sheriff here had both guns fingerprinted. Turns out the only print on the trigger of that MP-25 was Tiny Tim's. There's no way you pulled that trigger."

The ghost of Disco Donnie flickers and he presses both hands on his stomach. "I told you! I wasn't lyin'." He flickers again. "Geez, I feel funny."

"It gets better, Donnie. We found Tiny Tim, and I got him to confess." It seems like mentioning

Shelly would be counterproductive, so I leave that tidbit to be lost to the ages.

"That son of a gun is still alive? Wow. He used to smoke two packs a day."

"Trust me, Donnie, that bad habit caught up with him." Gesturing toward Erick, I point to his phone. "Sheriff Harper, can you play the confession?"

He pulls out his phone, scrolls through the recordings, and plays the confession for Donnie.

As Disco Donnie listens to the raspy, aged voice of his once friend, his eyes get a little misty. He nods in agreement with Tim Rosacker's version of events as the recording plays. Thankfully, the locked-on sheriff noticed me leaving Shelly out of my version of events, and pauses the track before Tim makes his last declaration of doing right by Shelly and the boys.

Donnie's already fading fast by the time we reach the end of the recording.

"It's time for you to let go, Donnie. You've been cleared of Lindy McElroy's murder. And you and Fred made your peace a long time ago. You can finally let go. I hope you got people waiting for you on the other side."

The film-school dropout in me swells with pride as I watch the darkened bank transform into a 1970s discotheque. The mirror ball on the ceiling twirls and the sparkling shards of light meld with Donnie's spirit as he fades out to take his last boogie on the disco 'round.

Oh yeah.

Fred watches from the shadows as Donnie disappears beyond the veil. His hope dares to bloom and he drifts forward. "Do you think you can really help me?"

Turning toward the spirit of the security guard, I keep my answer honest but hopeful. "In the end, it's up to you, Fred. Let me tell you what we uncovered."

Our small group settles in for the next stage of our operation. Stellen is kind enough to bring Yolo and Erick up to speed, while I prep Fred.

"Fred, have you ever heard of the butterfly effect?"

He floats aimlessly, as he searches his fading memories. "Is it a book?"

"No, well, I don't know. They did make a movie, so anything's possible. It's a concept that originated from Chaos theory. The butterfly effect refers to the interconnectedness of everything on our planet. The theory loosely means if a butterfly flaps its wings in the Amazon, it can trigger a sequence of events that could eventually lead to an avalanche which could kill a skier in the Rocky Mountains."

Fred shakes his head. "That sounds pretty far-fetched."

"Maybe, but the idea that every action has a re-action that technically causes a chain of events to occur isn't that hard to believe, is it?"

He wags his head back and forth. "I s'pose not."

"What I'm getting at, Fred, is that you blame yourself for Lindy McElroy's death because you hesitated that day in the bank."

He zooms toward me and shakes his finger adamantly. "It is my fault. I did hesitate. If I'd shot that Tiny Tim, Lindy McElroy would still be alive."

Shrugging my shoulders, I lift my hands and sigh. "Possibly. Although, you could have missed, and Tiny Tim would've shot her, anyway. The bottom line is, we don't know what could've happened. We only know what did happen. But your actions put something in motion. An entire sequence of events in the McElroys' lives."

Yolo presses her hands together and swallows hard.

Part of me wants to lay out every piece of the puzzle, but my brief experience with Fred leads me to believe he'll get bogged down in the negativity and not see the good. I think this is a situation where it's better to skip ahead. "I want you to meet someone, Fred."

His eyes trace the faces of everyone in the circle, and I gesture for Yolo to get to her feet.

Stellen pats her leg supportively. She stands and looks left and right.

"Yolo, Fred is right there, just behind Stellen."

She smiles and turns toward what she sees as an empty space.

"Fred Clements, I'd like you to meet Yolonda McElroy Olson. She's the great-granddaughter of Lindy McElroy."

Fred's heavily lidded eyes widen and his apparition glows the brightest I've seen yet. "Lindy's kid did okay?"

Not really the point, and I'm not about to get Fred sidetracked. "Things ended up exactly as they were supposed to, Fred. Yolo is a brilliant scientist and a genius inventor. She graduated from high school early and got accepted into a special program at MIT. For all we know, she could be the person who discovers time travel."

Yolo turns toward me and raises one fingerless-gloved finger. "Technically, time travel has already been discovered. Particle theory . . . Well, not to get sidetracked. The point is, we need to perfect the calculations of space travel so that when we move molecules through time, we can predict the space where they will land."

The rest of us exchange confused glances, and I

reply. "I'll take your word for it, Yolo."

She covers her perfect little mouth with one hand and nods. "Got it. Not really the point of your speech."

"What I'm trying to say is that Yolo was adopted by a loving family who was grateful for a child. They created this beautiful environment for her to be the best version of herself. Your hesitation in the bank over fifty years ago resulted in this. I know you carry guilt for what happened, but can you see another side of it now?"

Big salty ghost tears are rolling down Fred's ruddy cheeks. "I still feel like I need to apologize to her."

"All right. Stellen, can you help Yolo connect with Fred?"

Stellen gets to his feet, steps behind Yolo and lifts both of her arms toward the approaching specter.

"Now, Fred, go ahead and take hold of Yolo's hands."

He gently grips her fairy fingers in his meaty paws, and she shivers. "It's a pleasure to meet you, Yolonda McElroy Olson. So sorry I wasn't able to save your great-grandmother. But you turned out to be a lovely woman. If I manage to make it to the other side, I'll be sure to tell her just that."

I jump in as an afterlife interpreter and share

Fred's heartfelt message with Yolo. The ghost bumps on her arms dissipate as she sinks into his ethereal grasp. "Fred, I can't technically see you, but I can feel you. And I want you to know, I forgive you. I forgive you, and I want you to tell my great-grandmother that, too."

Now everyone's crying. Even Erick has to wipe an errant tear from his cheek.

A vast green meadow opens behind Fred. A golf cart pulls up, driven by a man I don't recognize —but who bears a strange familiarity.

"Fred, I think that's your ride."

Fred reluctantly drops Yolo's hands and turns in the direction I'm pointing.

"Jed Willoughby? Is that you? I haven't seen you on the links in a month of Sundays."

"Come on, Fred. You're late for your tee time."

Fred takes a step toward the waiting cart, but turns and glances over his shoulder. "Thank you, Mitzy Moon. I never thought I'd see this day."

Swiping at my traitorous tears, I swallow hard. "You keep a backgammon table warm for Silas Willoughby. I'm sure he'll outlive me, but eventually he'll be joining you."

Fred's eyes brighten, and he laughs with the lightness of an unburdened spirit. He slips into the golf cart.

The vision, and Fred Clements vanish.

*CHAPTER 18*

It's been a long and exhausting day. My need for peace and quiet supersedes my desire to hang out with Erick—or spill secrets. Stellen offers to give Yolo a ride home, and Erick and I head toward Main Street. He walks me to the corner and kisses me goodnight before returning to the station.

Don't get me wrong, it's a great kiss. It definitely makes me reconsider my choices, but in the end the exhaustion trumps the tingles.

The night air is icy, but now I can't bring myself to head inside. As tired as I feel and as much as I love Grams, I need a little break from ghosts right now.

Pulling up the zipper on my puffy jacket, I head down the embankment toward the thawing shores of our great lake.

Tomorrow is going to be a lot. I'm looking forward to celebrating my birthday with my wonderful family and what I'm sure will be many new friends. However, part of my heart longs for the simplicity of eating cake in bed with my mother.

They say time heals all wounds, but I haven't found that to be true. Time dulls the pain and changes the perspective, but the gash that was left in my heart when Coraline Moon was taken from me will never truly heal. I don't think I can handle all of tomorrow's hype on my own.

Without a conscious awareness of my actions, I see my phone in my hand, and a welcome voice pours from the speaker.

"Good evening, Mitzy. I hope the lateness of your call is not cause for alarm."

"Silas. It's so good to hear your voice. It's been the craziest day."

He gently coaxes the details from me and offers touches of wisdom and encouragement as needed. "I'm pleased you were able to help Mr. Clements. His spirit deserves peace."

"I agree. I think everyone can use a little peace every now and then."

"And is that the true purpose of your call, Mizithra?"

Uh oh, formal name territory. He's onto me. "I knew you'd get to the heart of the matter sooner or later, Silas. I'm sure you're aware of the grand festivities Grams has planned for tomorrow."

He harrumphs and chuckles softly. It's easy to picture him smoothing his mustache with a thumb and forefinger. "Your grandmother's spirit is not easily contained. She has gone to a great deal of effort and I hope you will enjoy yourself."

Wrapping my arms around my knees, I shudder in the face of the frozen lake's gaze. "I want to. I actually want to. I just don't think I can take all of that energy. You know what I mean? I kinda want to seal myself off from all the psychic hits and unwanted extrasensory information."

"I understand perfectly. Allow me to offer a solution."

A sense of relief seeps into my shoulders. "Thank you, Silas. I knew I could count on you."

"It is not I on whom you shall count. In this matter, you must perform the technique on yourself. You must never give your power away. You may choose when to use it or when to turn down the volume, but you must never allow another person to control your gifts."

There's a deeper message in there somewhere, but the weight of the day is tugging at my eyelids. I have no interest in delving into the depths of this lesson. "I understand. What should I do?"

"Get to your feet."

How does he know I'm sitting down? No time for that. I'll skip that question and stand. "All right. I'm ready."

"Place your right hand in front of your body, just below your belly button. Turn your palm up as though you're scooping something."

"Got it."

"Now scoop your right hand slowly upward all the way to the top of your head, slowly inhaling. As your hand moves, visualize closing the receptors in your body by choice. Remain in control. You are consciously making this decision."

As my hand moves upward, something shifts. "I feel something."

"Well done. Perform the movement two more times, using the same visualization each time. After the third motion is complete, you may say aloud, if you wish, 'It is done.'"

I repeat the gesture, as I've been instructed, and when I finish I say aloud, "It is done."

"You should be ready to face the day tomorrow with renewed inner strength. I look forward to my part in the momentous occasion's busy schedule."

As I'm about to end the call, a sudden concern pops to the forefront. "Wait, how do I turn it off? Or am I turning it back on?"

"Ah, yes. Simply reverse the motions and visualize yourself opening up to all the messages the universe has to offer. Once again, you are in control of the flow. You are not the tool, you wield the tool."

"Thank you, Silas. Thank you for taking my call. I'm sorry to have bothered you so late at night."

"Your calls are never a bother, Mizithra. Sleep well, and I wish you the happiest of birthdays."

My attempt to sneak into the bookstore via the alley door is a double epic fail.

"Ree-ow." Soft but condescending.

"Mitzy! We've been worried sick! What happened at the bank?"

Crouching down to scratch Pyewacket between his black-tufted ears, I feel calm flowing over me. "It's nice to see you guys. It has been THE craziest day. Follow me upstairs and I'll tell you as much of the story as I can before I crash out."

Our strange animal-human-ghost trio meanders up to the apartment. I barely have the energy to take off my coat. Tonight is definitely going to be a "sleep in my clothes" kind of night.

I share the highlights of the story with Grams, and drift off to sleep as she's singing my praises.

"Oh Mitzy, I'm so proud of you. You really helped—"

. . .

A SPARKLE OF SUNLIGHT dances across my eyelids a moment before a hungry caracal head butts me.

"Easy does it, son. I'm awake. I'm awake. Give me a second to take care of my human business, and I'll pour your Fruity Puffs. Deal?"

"Re-ow." Thank you.

As I stumble down the spiral staircase, Grams zooms up to greet me. "Happy birthday! I wanted to be the first."

"Well, technically, Silas wished me a happy birthday last night, but that was before midnight, so I suppose it doesn't count. I'll give you the official title of first birthday wisher."

She claps her hands as though it's an actual contest. "You better jump in the shower. Odell slipped a note under the door and he's planning to have breakfast with you this morning. I'm sure you'll want to look your best."

"I'll agree to wash my face and even comb my hair, but there's no way I'm taking a shower before breakfast. We'll deal with that when I get back. I assume you'll have an outfit laid out for me?"

She places a bejeweled hand over her mouth and giggles. "I'll see what I can do."

Filling Pye's bowl, I complete my task and back away. While he indulges in one of his favorite pastimes, I trudge upstairs and drag a brush through my hair.

Yesterday's T-shirt will have to do. Throwing on my jacket, I attempt to escape before Grams can scold me.

No such luck.

"Honestly, Mitzy. You have a closet literally overflowing with gorgeous couture. You could at least put on a fresh shirt."

"I'll be back soon, Grams. And then I'm all yours. You can dress me up like a little dolly and tell me to do whatever you want with my hair. Just let me enjoy my birthday breakfast in peace, all right?"

Her aura practically bursts with joy. "Oh, all right. I'll see you soon."

When I walk into the diner, Odell offers me a spatula salute through the orders-up window. And Tally's smile beams brightly as she brings two cups of coffee to the table, while Odell follows with our breakfasts. He's made me my favorite, of course. But I'm eager to discover what's on his plate.

"Chicken fried steak, two eggs over easy, and a side of whole wheat toast. Good to know, Gramps."

He winks and smiles. "Happy birthday, Mitzy. Or should I say, world's greatest granddaughter."

I offer a formal nod. "I'll accept the title."

He chuckles and we both dive into our delicious fare.

Odell wipes the corner of his mouth with a thin

paper napkin and gazes across the table. "So, how long have you known?"

I attempt to paint my features in a portrait of innocence, but there is no fooling Odell. "I mean, I think I've known the whole time."

He lifts his mug in a toast. "Here's to some of the best acting I've seen since Myrtle Isadora herself."

"I hope so. I really didn't want to spoil her fun."

"Don't worry, many have tried, none succeeded. When Myrtle Isadora gets her mind on something, come hell or high water, there's no changin' it."

We clink our mugs and enjoy a humorous toast at my grandmother's expense.

"I'm not sure what part you played in all of it, but thanks. It's my first actual birthday party since—"

A strong hand reaches across the table and lovingly pats my fingers. "Happy to do it. I'd do anything for you. You know that, right?"

The protection that Silas taught me last night is doing its job. I can sense the tenderness in Odell's comment, but it doesn't hit me in the gut as hard as I know it usually would. Good news. I might actually make it through this day in one piece. "Thank you. You know I'd do the same for you."

Breakfast ends too soon. I give Odell an enormous hug before reluctantly returning to the book-shop to take my role as Ghost-ma's plaything.

THERE'S NO DENYING the rejuvenating properties of a luxurious steam shower and eucalyptus-scented bath products. By the time I towel off and rake my fingers through my wet hair, my worries are soothed and I'm ready for anything Grams is going to throw at me.

"Good! Get your rear end in that closet and be prepared for a fashion show!"

Blerg.

"I gave you three options, which I think are quite reasonable considering how excited I am about this day." Ghost-ma hovers eagerly above her selections.

"You and I have very different definitions of reasonable, Isadora."

Grams flits about the closet like the fairy god-mother she is. "Start here!"

The first contraption I'm forced into makes me look exactly like a giant blob of cotton candy with a head stuck on top.

"It's lovely!"

"Gimme a break. The only person who would think this is lovely is a sugar-addicted toddler. I'm sorry, Grams, but it's a hard pass."

"All right. On to the next one!"

I extract myself from the frothy gown and pick up a slinky red number. This dress is less grandiose, but, in my opinion, it leaves far too *little* to the imagination.

"Nonsense. You have a dashing figure. There's nothing wrong with flaunting it." She circles around me like a hyperactive judge at a dog show.

"Once again, I don't share your opinion on the flaunting front. Plus, it's not exactly warm outside. I realize all of you almost-Canadians think that anything above freezing is suntanning weather, but I'm not there yet." I peel off the *Lady in Red* wardrobe and wait for further instruction.

"Well, I guess we're down to the last option. Looks like you'll be wearing this one, whether you like it or not."

"Don't get ahead of yourself, Isadora." Lifting the hanger and scanning the last item, the nicest thing I can say about the final selection is that it has pant legs. "A jumpsuit? What am I, five?"

"Jumpsuits are the height of fashion. That was custom made by one of the finest designers in New York City. Give it a fair chance." Grams zips me up in the back and I tug at the puffy shoulders.

"It seems a little frou-frou."

"It's called style, dear. Get on board."

Turning back and forth in front of the full-

length mirror, there is something nice about the way
the tapered pants give the illusion of long legs. I'm
not entirely sure I'm in love with the bright-red hue
of the fabric or the pin-cherry-printed top, but as I
gaze at the empty padded mahogany bench in the
center of my enormous closet, I'm out of options.

"Don't you just love it?"

"I don't. It seems a bit snug, and the pants are
too long."

"Hardly! Slip into those silver heels I selected."

Of course, I forgot the *pièce de résistance* to any
of Ghost-ma's getups: heels!

"Now, Mitzy, I know ten women who would—"

"I know, I know. Ten women who would kill to
wear these shoes for five minutes."

Grams crosses her arms and her coral lips purse
into a pout. "Well, it's true."

I buckle on the strappy silver shoes and twist in
front of the mirror. I feel silly, but I look nice. And it
is my birthday.

"You look fantastic. And you deserve to feel like
the Pin Cherry princess on your birthday!"

"Grams! Get out of my head. Just because I'm
allowing you to pick out my outfit, doesn't mean I'm
allowing you to pick my brain."

She giggles wildly. "You're such a card!"

"Well, it looks like the clothing dilemma has
been solved. Now what?"

"Let's get that hair blown out and shining like the moon." She snickers at her own clever quip. "And, you absolutely have to wear some makeup today."

Once I've carried out the orders of my otherworldly master, an unexpected arrival catches me off guard.

Twiggy's voice crackles over the intercom. "Hey, kid, you've got a fan club or something waiting for you."

My thoughts jump to the ragtag bunch of snowmobilers I met last winter, but that definitely doesn't make sense.

"Time to head downstairs, sweetie. Let's get your party started."

"One last thing." Hurrying to the jewelry box, I slip out the dreamcatcher necklace that belonged to my mother and clasp it around my neck. She may be gone, but at least she'll be with me in spirit.

Grams sniffles and dabs at her eyes. "Oh, Mitzy."

I swallow hard and stuff down all the feels. "Let's do this."

## CHAPTER 19

WALKING ACROSS THE LOFT, I take a moment to catch my breath and center myself. Today is about fun. It's important to keep a positive attitude and go with the flow.

"That's the spirit, dear."

"Grams!" There's no point wasting my breath. I head downstairs and it's hard to admit, but I'm pleased when I watch Erick's mouth drop open and his eyes widen with anticipation. "Wow! You look amazing."

I stop just before the "No Admittance" chain and twist left and right. "Thank you. I've been dressed by the best ghost stylist in all of Pin Cherry."

Stellen and Yolo get a chuckle from that comment, but Erick is still admiring the merchandise.

Rather than tempt fate, I unhook the chain, hurry to the bottom step, and hook it back up again before the alarm can sound. "So what happens now?"

Erick pulls a piece of paper from the back pocket of his "just right" jeans and fans it in the air. "Maybe you should take a look at this."

He hands me the 3 x 5 card and I read it aloud.

> "Come to the one place where
>    wheels repair
> All kinds of legs, fins, and beaks
>    with flair."

"What is this? A riddle?"

Yolo bounces up and down on her toes and adjusts her festive bandolier. Rather than ammunition, her steampunk version holds candies, lip gloss, and small tools. "It's a scavenger hunt!"

"Oh, I get it now. We have to solve the riddle to get the next clue?"

Stellen smiles. "You got it, sis. What's your answer?"

I read the riddle silently a couple more times, and then it hits me. "Wheels! Like on a wheelchair. It's gotta be Doc Ledo. Let's head over to the veterinary clinic."

Erick leads the way and we all follow him out to his Nova parked in the alley.

As per usual, he drives his personal vehicle with far more abandon than his police cruiser. Speed limits may be stretched or possibly broken, and brakes are only used as an afterthought. We arrive at the vet's office in record time.

The four of us rush through the front door, full of giggles and energy.

Doc Ledo rolls out from the back room and offers a wave. "So the game is afoot, eh?"

We return the wave, and Stellen replies. "Yep. Mitzy figured out the first clue, no problem. Do you have the next one for us?"

He crosses his arms and shakes his head. "I was instructed to offer no assistance. The four of you are used to solving mysteries, right? You better get crackin'."

Our shoulders sag and we look at each other in confusion. I sum up our conundrum. "So we don't just have to solve the riddle. We have to figure out where the next clue is once we get to the place the riddle takes us?"

Doc Ledo nods. "That sounds about right. I wish you luck. Gotta get back to work." And without further ado, he wheels into the back and leaves us unaided.

"Since it's Mitzy's birthday, let's assume all the

clues will have to do with her." Erick shrugs his shoulders and we all nod in helpless agreement. "So, how many times have you been here?"

Chewing the inside of my cheek, I rifle through my memories. "Quite a few times. Pyewacket is always getting himself into trouble."

Stellen chuckles. "Accurate."

Yolo raises her hand, as though we're in a classroom, but proceeds without waiting to be acknowledged. "Maybe it has to be something important. Not just a routine visit. How about the first time you were here?"

When the memory of Pyewacket taking a bullet for me and my father hits me in the gut, I'm glad to be feeling that memory through a filter. Once again, I'm thankful for the protection Silas taught me last night. "Wow, I can't believe I almost forgot about Pye getting shot."

Erick nods excitedly. "That's right. You insisted on staying at the animal hospital with your cat, like a freaky cat lady."

I punch him playfully on the arm. "Hey, that cat saved my life. I'm sure if your precious little potbelly pig, Casserole, had done something like that for you, you would've followed him to the ends of the earth."

He nods. "Precious Casserole, God rest him."

Stellen waves his hands eagerly. "That's gotta

be it. Focus up, everyone. If Pyewacket was shot, there must've been a surgery and recovery. If you were staying with him, maybe the clue is in the recovery room."

Yolo squeezes an arm around Stellen's shoulders. "Dude! You're onto something!"

We all rush toward the hallway, and Stellen, who interned at this clinic, leads the way.

Outside of the recovery room, there's an envelope taped right below the placard.

Stellen pulls the envelope from the wall and hands it to me. "We found it. Read the next clue!"

It's fun. I'm allowing myself to be swept up in the moment. I wish my mother could be here, but I'm lucky to have such a wonderful group of friends to share this special day with me. Time to let the past drift away and enjoy everything that's special about the here and now. Opening the envelope, I fan the next clue and wink at Erick. "You ready, Sheriff?"

He winks back and claps his hands. "I was born ready, Moon."

As I read the second clue aloud, my face shifts to an unbecoming shade of red, which closely matches the pants portion of my pantsuit.

*"You once stormed a tin castle*
*within our walls,*
*In an effort to escape the law's*
*eyeballs."*

"A tin castle?" Erick shakes his head. "There aren't any castles in Pin Cherry. Do you think we have to drive out of town?"

Stellen and Yolo offer a few suggestions while I dwell in embarrassed silence. Finally, all eyes turn toward me.

"I know that look, Moon. Spill." Erick crosses his arms in that yummy way that makes his biceps bulge, and I'm powerless to resist.

"I don't know how you guys got this information, but there was this one time at the grocery store when I had a little run-in with Deputy Paulsen. After I dropped a really solid burn, and I wanted to get out of the store before she could think of a comeback . . . I was running kind of fast down one of the aisles, and I turned and slammed right into a tower of cans. I hit the ground. The cans hit the ground. It was mortifying."

Everyone enjoys a hearty laugh at my expense.

Erick raises his hand in the air to ignite the charge. "To the Piggly Wiggly!"

Once we reach the store, I'm forced to access a

quick psychic replay to see if I can find additional clues.

"Where was the tower, Mitzy?" Yolo gently asks.

"It was right up front. You know, one of those holiday endcaps."

"What was in the cans?" Stellen leans forward eagerly.

"I think it was pumpkin."

We race to the baking aisle and crouch down in front of the pie fillings. There, below the cans of pumpkin puree, is another telltale envelope.

Yolo squeals with excitement. "We found it!"

She pulls the envelope from the shelf and hands it to me. But I wave it away and point to her. "No. You found it. You read this one."

Yolo opens the envelope, fans the card dramatically, and clears her throat.

> *"All these words are taken without*
> *pay,*
> *But none are stolen or given away."*

I can't make heads or tails of it. "Words without pay?" The four of us exchange shrugs.

"Could it be the newspaper?" Erick offers his idea, with little conviction.

Shaking my head, I sigh. "No. Reporters are

paid for their stories, and people have to buy news-papers. So the 'without pay' part doesn't apply."

Stellen lifts his finger. "If people don't pay, but they don't steal and they aren't given, how do they get the words?"

My eyes sparkle with excitement. "I've got it! The library! People check out the books. They don't steal them or buy them."

Erick gestures toward the front door of the Piggly Wiggly. "Back in the car, everyone."

I argue for a stop off at the patisserie for a flaky pastry recharge, but the team is too excited to enter-tain a distraction. Yolo offers me one of her candies as a consolation prize.

You know me—of course I take it.

The four of us run up the steps and burst through the front door, but as we stand in the vast atrium, the sheer weight of our search dampens the spirit.

Yolo says what we're all thinking. "It could be anywhere. I wouldn't even know where to start."

Erick paces in front of the entrance.

Yolo bounces on her tiptoes and taps a finger on her bottom lip.

Stellen and I lock eyes, as though some step-sib-ling mind meld can save us.

Wait, it's actually working.

Stellen smiles, and his green eyes twinkle. "It's all about you, right, Mitzy?"

I nod.

"So your foundation rebuilt the entire library after the tornado, but you added a special wing for curated displays."

"You're right! Let's start there."

We hurry toward the displays, and, as we pass through the entrance to the Duncan-Moon exhibit hall, my heart fills with pride. There's a lovely display honoring my grandfather, Cal Duncan, and his contribution to the railroad industry in Pin Cherry Harbor. One of my grandmother's wedding gowns is lit up like a Christmas tree, and there's a lengthy explanation of her many philanthropic ventures in the community. But when I see the one-of-a-kind flapper dress that used to reside in my apartment, glittering in its newfound home, my heart skips a beat.

One of my favorite ancestors, Sidney Jensen, left her mark on history. The first female jazz saxophone player, and quite a femme fatale in the 1920s. She fell in with the wrong crowd when she became a gangster's moll, but I happen to know the ghostly end of that story, and it warms my heart to see this memorabilia.

"The saxophone! I don't know why, but I think

it might have something to do with that instrument."

My three teammates turn, and we carefully approach the display. The saxophone hangs on a stand inside a glass case. No envelope is visible.

Yolo pats my shoulder. "It was a good idea."

Erick drops to the ground, rolls onto his back, and slides under the display like a mechanic on a creeper. "Found it."

We all clap.

He rolls out and hands me the envelope.

"New rule. Finders keepers. You found it, you read it."

Erick opens the envelope, scans the card, and chuckles.

> *"Here you were once arrested for*
> *being a fake.*
> *A few donations and a speech cut*
> *you a break."*

He flashes his eyebrows. "Do you remember?"

Stellen steps forward and grabs my arm. "I remember. It was that day you came to the high school and pretended to be a student from the community college. You defended me when they picked on me in health class." His voice catches in his throat, and his eyes glisten with emotion.

Bumping my shoulder against his, I grin. "Yeah, I felt like crap when my cover was blown and the sheriff tossed me in cuffs."

Erick throws his hands in the air. "How am I coming out of this thing the bad guy? You were impersonating a teacher at a high school!"

"I was on a case, Sheriff."

Stellen throws an arm around my shoulders. "I'm glad you got arrested that day, sis. I had no idea how things would turn out between us. But I knew you were good people."

My cheeks flush with color. "Aw, shucks."

Erick shoves the envelope in his pocket. "Looks like we're off to the high school, gang."

The high school has played a role in several of my investigations. But since Stellen brought back the memory of my first visit there. I might know where to start our search.

Once inside, I share my theory with the crew. "Since the clue has to do with the first time I was at the school. I think we should start in the nurse's office. She was the person I was shadowing when I was pretending to help with the health classes."

We head into the nurse's office and begin searching randomly.

Yolo stops, tilts her head to the side, and points. "Those computers are new. Were they part of your donation?"

I rush toward the shiny new screens. "They were!" Searching around the new computer, I find the envelope taped to the back of the computer screen. "I finally found one!"

They all gesture for me to rip it open.

> *"This is the place where you took a*
> *risky cheap shot.*
> *It was almost as though you wanted*
> *to get caught."*

"Um, this is gonna be tough. People tell me I take a lot of risks."

Stellen nods. "That's actually true."

"Rude."

Erick rubs his hands along his jaw. "I can really only think of one cheap shot that resulted in you getting caught."

My eyes widen. "Oh. Yeah. Sorry about that. Again."

Stellen and Yolo gaze back and forth between Erick and me, and Yolo asks, "What are you talking about, Erick?"

He sucks air in between his teeth and shakes his head. "Mitzy was working undercover as a bartender at Final Destination. Before I knew what she was up to, I came in and saw her there—in a wig. To keep me from blowing her cover, she punched me in the face."

Stellen and Yolo gasp simultaneously. "What did you do?"

I throw my arms in the air and wave wildly. "Let's not get sidetracked, gang. We have our next clue. We know we're going to Final Destination. Load up."

The junior sleuths continue to mumble as we head back out to the Nova.

As soon as we walk through the creaking front door of the town's only dive bar, Lars shouts a hello and points to the minors. "For the record, Sheriff, they came in with you."

Erick nods and waves the owner's worry away with a quick gesture. "Absolutely. We're just here to find a clue in this crazy scavenger hunt."

Lars puts both of his large hands on the bar and takes a deep breath. "Well, you won't get any help from me. Or at least that's what I was told."

Leaning one elbow on the bar, I smile up at him. "And nobody crosses Twiggy. Right?"

He nods firmly. "Darn right."

Stellen circles the pool tables, grabs a handful of stale bar mix, and munches on it while he thinks. "Where did the, um, incident take place, Erick?"

Erick walks toward one of the barstools. "Right here."

Yolo rushes forward and feels around underneath the seat.

I step toward the action. "Incorrect, Sheriff. You were sitting on this stool." I reach underneath and secure the envelope. Waving it back and forth to the rest of the crew, I announce, "That's two for me."

Stellen leans in. "Yep. Read it."

> *"Ancient narwhal tusk and a deadly*
> *rival.*
> *Your study group was a means of*
> *survival."*

The mention of the narwhal tusk brings a sick swirl of nausea to my stomach. Anytime a memory of Rory Bombay surfaces, it's decidedly unpleasant.

Erick sees the look on my face and places a comforting arm around my shoulders. "Don't think about the bad stuff. Just think about what the clue means."

"Copy that. I guess it's probably the community college. Since it mentions the study group, that must refer to the students. And I was pretending to be a student there at the time."

Stellen chuckles. "Again? You pretended to go there twice?"

I shake my head. "You're such a little brother."

He smiles proudly. "Okay, let's all go to college."

Erick drives us over.

Locked. Closed for spring break. We got lucky at the high school. There was a crew there repainting the hallways. No such luck at Birch County Community College.

Yolo sidles up next to me and points to her bandolier.

A thrill and a giggle grip me. "Sheriff, you better look the other way."

Erick scrunches up his face, but it only takes him a second to clock our intentions. "I'm not involved."

"Copy that."

Yolo hands me a tension wrench and a rake—I won't even ask why she has them—and in less than a minute, I'm in. Thanks must be offered to my horrible foster brother, Jarrell. He did teach me a few useful things amidst all the cons.

"Looks like this door is open." I announce my "find" loudly, and Erick reluctantly follows us into the administration building.

After a few dead ends, I mention that the case was the one where the professor was murdered. "I bet it's in Professor Klang's old office."

Since I'm the only one who knows where that is, I lead the team. As we round the last corner, Yolo rushes ahead and snatches the envelope tucked under the nameplate of the new professor. "That's two for me, too!"

I offer her a wink. "Great minds. What can we say?"

She giggles and pulls out the clue. "It says this is the final clue."

> *"Now, back to the place where it all*
> *began.*
> *A ghost, a cat, and cranky human."*

Four voices unite, "Bell, Book & Candle!"

CHAPTER 20

INSTEAD OF DRIVING STRAIGHT BACK to my book-shop, Erick parks in the small parking lot beside the Duncan Restorative Justice Foundation. Weird, right?

"Is there a reason you parked so far away from my store, Sheriff?"

He purposely avoids my gaze, mumbles something unintelligible under his breath, and hops out of the car. He circles around and opens my door while Stellen and Yolo wait for me to slide the seat up so they can tumble out of the back.

There is an eager anticipation humming through my cohorts.

Fine. I'll let sleeping dogs lie.

As we round the corner onto First Avenue, my

father and Amaryllis race down the front steps of the foundation and look as though they've seen Sasquatch when they spot me on the sidewalk.

"Mitzy! How's my favorite daughter?"

Amaryllis rushes toward me, unzips my coat, and lifts my arms up. "The jumpsuit is gorgeous! I couldn't quite picture it from Isadora's written description, but it really is breathtaking."

A round of happy birthdays and hugs follows their hurried comments. When I move to continue toward the bookshop, Amaryllis scoops my arm into the crook of her elbow and squeezes. The gold flecks in her eyes catch the late afternoon light, and big auburn curls poke out from beneath her stocking cap.

"All right, what are you guys up to?"

My father dons his best poker face. "Up to? Can't a father wish his daughter happy birthday?"

The awkward silence is interrupted by the strains of a famous '80's song. Amaryllis claps her mittened hands together and tugs me forward. "It's go time!"

As we surge forward, the chorus of "Hungry Like the Wolf" echoes down the street.

Pointing toward the ruckus, I ask, "So, it sounds like there's a DJ. Will there also be a dance floor?"

My posse giggles, and when we reach the

corner of First and Main, my eyes nearly pop out of my head. Apparently, the scavenger hunt was a total decoy. While we were away, an enormous tent popped up. The sounds of music, laughter, and several luscious aromas are wafting from within.

"How in the world? It would've taken like a hundred people to get this together while we were gone."

Biker boots stomp out of the tent, and Twiggy shakes her severe grey pixie cut. "Try two hundred, kid. Your grandmother spared no expense."

And with that, she holds open the door of the beautiful tent and ushers me inside. A forest of sparkling trees, spaced between quite necessary propane heaters, illuminate the tent that engulfs the entire cul-de-sac next to my store.

"It's gorgeous! It's like a fairy wonderland." My gaze is drawn to the live band—not a DJ. "Wait! Is that Duran Duran?"

Twiggy puts a firm hand on my shoulder. "Not exactly. After their sixth refusal, Isadora got me onto finding a cover band. It's as close as I could get to the real thing."

Erick takes my hand and pulls me to the dance floor. "Is this one of your favorite bands or something?"

A warm memory floods in. "Not really, but I

told Grams a story about one of my favorite memories of my mother. I had the chickenpox, and she had to take a couple days off work, from both of her jobs. Which now I know must've been very hard on us financially. At the time, she never let on it was any problem. She got out an old stack of records, and she played her Duran Duran album over and over—dancing all silly to keep my spirits up and distract me from itching. I'm sure she played music from other bands, but this was the one that stuck." A tear springs to the corner of my eye. "Grams thought of everything."

Erick turns me to the left and points to the roof of the tent. "She really did."

The side of the tent facing the bookstore has a clear plastic roof. I'm sure people will assume it's so we can dance under the stars, but as I gaze through the 6 x 6 windows on the side of the bookshop. My heart melts with love. Grams is blowing me kisses through the slumped glass window pane.

Without thinking, I wave like an idiot and blow kisses back.

Tally approaches to wish me a happy birthday. "Who are you waving at?"

"Oh, no one. I just thought that bird was looking at me."

Erick pokes me in the side. And I immediately giggle.

"Well, happy birthday. Odell will be here any minute. He's closing the diner early today in honor of your birthday."

"Wow. Almost feels like a national holiday."

She chuckles. "As far as he's concerned, it is."

Before I get caught up in admiring the doppelgänger Duran Duran band, Erick steers me toward the buffet. "You better eat something. I understand your grandmother made an exception to her no alcohol policy, after significant pressure from Twiggy. And, if I know you, there'll be a lot of champagne heading downstream. You better get a base going."

Pushing up to my tiptoes, I plant a kiss on his cheek and wipe away the smudge of red lipstick. "You're not wrong."

Anne, from Bless Choux patisserie, is manning the buffet table. "All of your favorite desserts are stacked around your three-tier chocolate cake with salted-caramel filling and *dulce de leche* buttercream frosting."

I lean across the table and smile foolishly. "Have I told you how much I love you?"

She giggles and blushes. "Don't mention it. I was happy to do it."

"So what do we have here in the savory section?"

She walks us through the delectable options. "These are potato and cheese pierogies. Here is my interpretation of Far-East spiced meat pies, and these are macadamia nut and panko bread crumb John Dorys." She leans toward me and whispers, "It's fancy fish."

"Sounds great to me."

She moves down the buffet and introduces the various starchy side-dish options. "Orange and almond risotto, dauphinoise potatoes, and cheesy riced cauliflower."

There's a selection of vegetables, which don't really grab my interest, although the roasted Brussels sprouts with bacon are tempting.

"At the end, you'll find pumpernickel rolls, pull-apart buns, and a braided caraway loaf."

My mouth is watering, and I feel like one plate won't be enough. "You thought of everything."

Erick grabs a plate. "If you ask me, that's enough talking. Let's get to eating."

No one has to ask me twice. We pile our plates and grab a table beside the temporary dance floor. The tent is filling up, and well-wishers pass by the table every few seconds. I recognize most of the faces, but I can only produce names for a handful. Grams definitely invited everyone. Even though my list of acquaintances could barely fill a page—let alone an enormous tent.

The music rocks on, and Erick drags me onto the dance floor several times.

I even have to do something called a "chicken dance." Which is exactly what it sounds like.

Eventually, the Duran Duran wannabes play happy birthday, and Amaryllis serves up the delectable cake.

Just as I'm about to breathe a sigh of relief, a spotlight spins toward the crowd and nails me like an escaping convict in a silent movie. I reach for Erick's hand, but he's nowhere to be found.

A voice calls from the stage. "Ladies and gentlemen, please put your hands together for Sheriff Erick Harper." The Simon Le Bon lookalike hands the microphone to Erick as he steps into a second spotlight.

Oh no, what's happening? Is it what I think it is? Am I ready for this?

"Mitzy Moon, please join me on stage."

My feet are frozen in place.

Erick eggs on the crowd. "Let's give her a little encouragement, folks. You all remember how our Pin Cherry Princess likes to avoid the spotlight." The spotlight operator flicks the bright beam off and on, and the crowd roars with laughter.

I guess I better get up there. The longer I wait, the worse it's going to be.

As I move toward the front, applause erupts throughout the tent.

When I reach the stage, Silas steps from the

shadows and offers me a hand up the steps. I search his face for some clue as to what is about to happen, but he offers no hint.

Erick takes my hand and walks me to the center of the stage. "Well, Miss Moon. It's no secret how much you've helped the sheriff's department since you arrived in town."

My sense of humor defense mechanism is kicking in, and I can't stop myself from pulling the mic my direction. "Was that before or after you accused me of murder, Sheriff?"

The crowd's boisterous laughter bolsters my courage.

Erick comically hangs his head, but takes back the microphone. "I think it was the first time I laid eyes on you in the diner."

Oh dear. This is taking a turn, and I can't breathe.

He smiles out at the crowd. "Most of you probably think this is long overdue, but you all know me. Sometimes I can be a slow learner."

Another round of chuckles.

He reaches into his pocket with his right hand and pulls out a small flat box.

It's not the ring box I imagined, but who am I to judge? Let's see what he picked out.

Erick pops the box open toward the audience, and doesn't get on one knee.

I have to say, I'm a little disappointed. I've known him to be more chivalrous and romantic.

"Mitzy Moon," he turns the box toward me, "I'm making you an official honorary deputy of the Pin Cherry Harbor sheriff's department."

There's a moment of confusion in the crowd, but Amaryllis leaps to her feet clapping and everyone follows suit.

Confusion, mixed with disappointment, clouds my brain. I take the box, and I hope I smile, but when my ears hear the rest of his speech, I pray it's all a bad dream.

"Ladies and gentlemen, the Federal Bureau of Investigation has taken note of the work our sheriff's department has done with the help of civilian liaisons. I'll be heading to Quantico, Virginia, to lead an eight-week seminar assisting the Bureau in utilizing civilian liaisons to a more effective level. In exchange, I'll be involved in some training exercises, and our sheriff's department will receive some much-needed tech upgrades. However, your sheriff will get to be an instructor for several weeks. I'll leave you in the capable hands of acting Sheriff Paulsen and honorary deputy Moon, and I look forward to getting back to work with renewed purpose when I return."

The sound is fading from the room. All I can hear is a dull ringing. Someone takes my hand and leads me off the stage. A surge of excited citizens swarm around Erick, and I drift, alone, toward the tent's exit.

As soon as I pass through the front door of my beloved bookstore, the waterworks let loose. I fight to get my shoes off and abandon them in the stacks.

Running up to my apartment, I pull the candle handle and race inside. "Grams! Grams! Did you know he was going to do this? I can't believe you wouldn't tell me."

She swooshes from the window to my side. "Let me see the ring, sweetie!"

"Ring? What are you saying? It's a stupid deputy's badge. Something you'd give to an eager child."

I attempt to hand her the box, but it falls through her ethereal hand and hits the floor.

No one picks it up.

Sinking onto the settee, I sob into my hands.

"Deputy? It's not—"

I moan and echo her sentiment. "No, it's not."

Even with the protections in place, my heart aches, and my stomach is tied in knots.

The bookcase slides open behind me, but I refuse to turn.

"Isadora, if you're here, can we have a minute?" Erick's voice is soft and pleading.

Grams pops out of existence and he drops onto the settee next to me. He grips my hand and squeezes hard. "Hey, what's wrong?"

"What's wrong? Are you serious? You call me up on stage in front of the whole town, at my birthday party. Then you pull a box out of your pocket and make me an *honorary deputy*. What do you think is wrong?"

He drops my hand, heads into the bathroom, and retrieves a box of tissues. As I wipe my eyes, he explains. "Look, it wasn't a setup. I honestly thought you'd get a kick out of it. You're always teasing Paulsen about how you do her job better than she does, and the two of you will have to work together while I'm gone."

My chin shoots up and I stare daggers into his blue eyes. "Yeah, that's another thing. When were you planning on telling me?"

He squeezes my hand and shakes his head. "Hey, I know I took the coward's way out. I didn't want to tell you when we were kinda fighting. I didn't want to tell you after the whole bank heist scare—"

"I thought you were gonna propose, Erick. I feel like an idiot." I blow my nose loudly and throw the tissue on the floor.

He slips an arm around my shoulder. "Hey, we

said no surprises. Remember? I promised you that we would make that decision together, and it doesn't seem like you're ready."

I clench my jaw, but I can't argue with his logic.

"It seems like you've got a lot of things to think about. We can't be partially together. You need to decide if you're ready to trust me completely, and this opportunity seemed like a sign. To me, I mean. You'll get some space, and you can think about what you want in your life."

My gaze drops to the floor, and I suck in a ragged breath.

"Hey, everyone doesn't have to be married to be happy. And you don't have to share all of your secrets with me if it doesn't feel right. But I did a lot of thinking after the FBI offer came in, and I don't think I can be in a relationship where I only get to know a piece of my partner. I need my partner to trust me with her whole heart. Hopefully, this time apart gives you a chance to think about things—with no pressure. I'm not going anywhere—"

My voice is raw and angry. "False. You're going halfway across the country. For two months!"

He scoops me into his arms and kisses the top of my head. "What I mean is, my heart isn't going anywhere. I love you, Mitzy Moon. And I'm ready to give you every part of myself. But I'm also willing to give you the time to decide what you really want. I'd never force your hand."

I sigh and soften my tone. "When do you leave?"

"Tomorrow."

My eyelids jerk open, and there are no words.

He wipes a tear from my cheek and smiles in that way that melts my heart. "I didn't want to spoil your birthday by telling you before . . . Then, time kinda ran out."

Before I can protest, his lips are on mine, and I'm lost in a swirl of confusing emotions.

The good news: Ghost-ma planned the most amazing birthday party—ever! Plus, she surprised me beyond belief. Kudos to Grams.

The bad news: The other shoe dropped. Erick finally got tired of my coquettish games of evasion. It's time for me to face the music or fire the orchestra.

In other news: Don't tell Grams, but I think her serenity prayer is exactly what I need right now. I can't change the past, but if I can find the courage . . . There's still a chance to take the world as it is.

He's leaving town. He's not leaving me. He promised that his heart isn't going anywhere.

One day at a time. That's all any of us can handle.

. . .

*End of Book 18*

## A NOTE FROM TRIXIE

I know! I know! I can already see the emails. LOL! As Erick would say, "Sit tight." Mitzy Moon (*and Sheriff Too-Hot-To-Handle*) will be back in Book 19, and your heart will start beating again—I promise. I'll keep writing them if you keep reading . . .

The best part of "living" in Pin Cherry Harbor continues to be feedback from my early readers. Thank you to my alpha readers/cheerleaders, Angel (*who was furious with me*) and Michael (*who buried his rage*). HUGE thanks to my fantastic beta readers who continue to give me extremely useful and honest feedback: Veronica McIntyre and Nadine Peterse-Vrijhof (*also slightly miffed*). And big "small town" hugs to the world's best ARC Team – Trixie's Mystery ARC Detectives!

My fantastic editor Philip Newey definitely

sent me back to the drawing board on a critical scene. Thanks to him, I avoided a giant time fumble. I'd also like to give buckets of gratitude to Brooke for her tireless proofreading! (*Despite her jam-packed schedule.*) Any remaining errors are my own.

As usual, I turned to Morgan for gun facts, as well as various bus-related tidbits.

FUN FACT: One of my most prized books is an oversized, illustrated *Alice in Wonderland* from Grosset & Dunlap circa 1958.

My favorite line from this case: "If loving you is wrong, Mitzy Moon, I don't wanna be right." ~Erick

I'm currently writing book nineteen in the Mitzy Moon Mysteries series, and it's going to have a satisfying mystery and a hilarious switcheroo. Mitzy, Grams, and Pyewacket got into plenty of trouble in book one, *Fries and Alibis*. But I'd have to say that book three, *Wings and Broken Things*, is when most readers say the series becomes unputdownable.

I hope you'll continue to hang out with us.

*Trixie Silvertale* (March 2022)

Mitzy Moon Mysteries 19

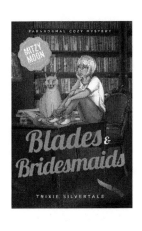

**A simple canoe trip. A deadly eco-warrior. Will our psychic sleuth be up a creek without a paddle?**

Mitzy Moon is a dry land kinda gal. Never in her life has she wanted to take an extended adventure in a tippy canoe. But when her newly engaged cousin calls for help, she'll have to put her faith in a snippy rival or risk losing everyone...

With a militant environmentalist stalking the bride-to-be and her maids on a camping trip, Mitzy is stuck with only mean-girl Deputy Paulsen as backup. After last-minute advice from Ghost-ma and her feisty feline, she heads deep into the wilderness to find the missing girls—with nothing but a tent and a flimsy plan.

Will Mitzy chance spilling her secrets, or turn turtle and transform the pending nuptials into a funeral?

*Blades and Bridesmaids* is the nineteenth book in the hilarious Mitzy Moon Mysteries paranormal cozy mystery series. If you like snarky heroines, supernatural intrigue, and a dash of romance, then you'll love Trixie Silvertale's cunning conundrum.

**Buy *Blades and Bridesmaids* to recycle a killer today!**

Grab yours here!
readerlinks.com/l/861835

Scan this QR Code with the camera on your phone. You'll be taken right to the Mitzy Moon Mysteries series page. You can easily grab any mysteries you've missed!

Once you're in the Club, you'll also be the first to receive updates from Pin Cherry Harbor and access to giveaways, new release announcements, short stories, behind-the-scenes secrets, and much more!

Scan this QR Code with the camera on your phone. You'll be taken right to the page to join the Club!

*THANK YOU!*

Trying out a new book is always a risk and I'm thankful that you rolled the dice with Mitzy Moon. If you loved the book, the sweetest thing you can do (*even sweeter than pin cherry pie à la mode*) is to leave a review so that other readers will take a chance on Mitzy and the gang.

Don't feel you have to write a book report. A brief comment like, "Can't wait to read the next book in this series!" will help potential readers make their choice.

★★★★★
Leave a quick review HERE
https://readerlinks.com/l/2234157
★★★★★

Thank you kindly, and I'll see you in Pin Cherry Harbor!

*Heists and Poltergeists: Paranormal Cozy Mystery*

*Blades and Bridesmaids: Paranormal Cozy Mystery*

More to come!

Trixie Silvertale grew up reading an endless supply of Lilian Jackson Braun, Hardy Boys, and Nancy Drew novels. She loves the amateur sleuths in cozy mysteries and obsesses about all things paranormal. Those two passions unite in her Mitzy Moon Mysteries, and she's thrilled to write them and share them with you.

When she's not consumed by writing, she bakes to fuel her creative engine and pulls weeds in her herb garden to clear her head (*and sometimes she pulls out her hair, but mostly weeds*).

Greetings are welcome:
trixie@trixiesilvertale.com

**BB** bookbub.com/authors/trixie-silvertale

**f** facebook.com/TrixieSilvertale

**O** instagram.com/trixiesilvertale

Manufactured by Amazon.ca
Bolton, ON

26871846R00152